RIVAL PRINCES

A FAIRYLAND ROMANCE

JAXON KNIGHT

GREY KELPIE STUDIO

Copyright © 2019 Jamie Sands

All rights reserved. No part of this book may be reproduced in any form or by any electronic or mechanical means, including information storage and retrieval systems, without permission in writing from the publisher, except by reviewers, who may quote brief passages in a review.

ISBN

epub 978-0-473-48461-3

Kindle: 978-0-47348462-0

Cover by Kat Savage

Edited by Emma Bryson

Printed in United States of America via Kindle Direct Publishing

Published by Grey Kelpie Studio

Visit https://www.facebook.com/JaxonKnightAuthor/

https://www.goodreads.com/author/show/19244965.Jaxon_Knight

https://www.bookbub.com/profile/jaxon-knight

1 / NATE

"You don't just walk into a prince role. No one does."

"Well, I did," Nate said with a shrug. He couldn't keep the smile off his face. He found himself gazing at the fan-made poster of Prince Valor, sword in hand, staring down a dragon.

He checked the time on his phone and winced. They needed to get going in the next couple of minutes if he was going to be on time.

Behind him, his best friend, Charlie, shook his head. "You're leading some kind of charmed life. That or you did a favor for the casting director."

Charlie and Nate had gone through school together. Charlie had always been taller than Nate right up to his final growth spurt in their senior year. Now he could look him in the eye. In high school, Charlie's red hair had been a marker of shame - and the reason Charlie said he never had a date - but Ed Sheeran had somehow made it cool recently, and the color highlighted his sparkling green eyes. Charlie was sitting on the old couch; the one Nate had owned since he moved out of his college dorm. Nate wondered if he should replace that thing once his first paycheck came in - he didn't have any furniture that wasn't thrifted or a hand me down.

"It's nothing like that." Nate rolled his eyes. "Besides, you know the whole park is squeaky clean. I have to sign a whole lot of papers about what I can and can't do as Prince Valor."

"Of course! You don't want anything inappropriate to happen on your watch."

Nate shuddered bodily at the thought. "You're right there.'

"But I guess there's a likeness, so I can see how they wanted you to be Valor." Charlie squinted at Nate. Uncomfortable under the scrutiny, Nate renewed his search for his newly issued Fairyland staff identification card.

"You really think so?" Nate hated sounding so needy, but he was a bundle of nerves, and he needed the reassurance.

"Yeah, you have those giant cartoon eyes, and you're all dark and handsome like he is," Charlie said.

Nate turned to look in the mirror. He could usually only see his faults. Like how he couldn't grow a proper beard, or his dry skin or the acne that he sometimes had over his forehead even though he wasn't a teenager anymore.

In the Fairyland cartoons Nate had watched growing up, Prince Valor was a tall, slim, muscular hero. He didn't get too much screen time in the movie he appeared in – it was really about Princess Patience – but he did rescue her from a dragon in a badass fight scene.

His own face wasn't as smooth as the cartoon character's, and he wasn't sure he had the right cheekbones. But his eyes were brown, and his hair was black. His skin was the right tone, a warm brown inherited from his Jamaican mother's side, and his jaw was okay.

"You have to be close shaved," Charlie said. "No five o'clock shadow."

"No concerns there," Nate turned to Charlie. "But we are in danger of running late. Can you please help me look for my ID?"

"If you'd just keep this place tidier, maybe you wouldn't lose things so much," Charlie grumbled. He stood and laughed, brandishing the card. "Ha – would you look at that – I was sitting on it!"

"Urgh, you're the worst." Nate held his hand out, bouncing on his toes a little. He slipped the lanyard around his neck so he couldn't lose it again.

"I'm the best, and you know it." Charlie winked one of his green eyes.

For a while, Nate had thought he had a crush on Charlie. But in the end, it had just been teen hormones, some confusion about coming out, and Charlie being his closest friend. There was no sexual chemistry between them.

It was Charlie's referral that had gotten Nate the audition in the first place. Charlie worked at Fairyland as well, in food preparation and counter service at one of the many restaurants.

Nate felt about to explode with nervous energy, so he rushed about cleaning up a few of the fast food wrappers and discarded soda cans that littered his apartment, stuffing them into a garbage bag. Then he looked around the room for something else to fix, biting his lip.

Charlie's expression softened. "Hey, dude, don't be nervous. Everything's gonna be fine."

Charlie put his hand on Nate's shoulder and rubbed it gently. "They won't even have you be Prince Valor today, anyway. They'll just show you the ropes, maybe get you to go along as a handler so you can see the others in action."

"Yeah, you're probably right." Nate stuffed the collected trash into the bin and straightened up, dusting off his hands. "We should go."

"Got your house keys?" Charlie asked, moving towards the door.

"Yep."

"Got your phone?"

Nate patted his pocket. "Yep."

"Well, Let's go then. And on the way, you can thank me for

keeping your life in order." Charlie spun his keys on his finger. They left the building and climbed into Charlie's rustbucket of a hatchback.

Nate licked his lips. He tapped his fingers on the armrest as Charlie drove. His stomach felt fluttery and tense at the same time. More than anything, he wanted to do well at this job.

As a kid, he'd adored the Fairyland movies: *Princess Patience's Challenge*, *Princess Honesty and the Witch*, the ones with the fairies in them. Well, all of them. He could remember each of the five times his mother had taken him to the park clearer than even his first day of school.

The first time he'd visited the park, he was six years old. His sister, Natasha, was eight. She was taller, so she could go on more of the rides, which had seemed terribly unfair. Nate had loved the spinning lily pads in the Enchanted Forest. He'd met Princess Honesty and Prince Valor. He'd eaten cotton candy and a hotdog. He'd ridden the kiddy coaster so many times that he'd worn himself out. He couldn't remember the fireworks show, but in the photos showed he was there, asleep in his mother's arms, clutching a stuffed unicorn.

He still had that first souvenir. Treasure the Unicorn had ignited his love for Fairyland merchandise. Now he was going to work there, he was even going to work alongside the person who *played* Treasure the Unicorn. Maybe he'd have to cover for Treasure the Unicorn? He didn't much like the idea of that hot fursuit in the summer.

Charlie shut off the engine and slapped the wheel, jarring Nate out of his reverie.

"Here we are," Charlie said. "Ready or not."

Nate briefly felt like he was going to vomit, but he clenched his teeth. He wasn't going to back out just because he was nervous.

Charlie took him in through the staff door. People were already queuing at the main gates, despite the park not opening for an hour. They went through the security checks and then to the head office to sign Nate in officially. There, Charlie handed him off to a serious-but-handsome staff member.

"Nate, meet Lennon. Lennon's going to guide you as you settle in and answer any questions. Lennon, this is Nathaniel. Don't let his good looks fool you, he's very nervous."

"Am not." Nate held out his hand to shake Lennon's. "Call me Nate. It's a pleasure to meet you, Lennon."

"Welcome. Don't worry, you have nothing to be nervous about." Lennon smiled warmly and shook Nate's hand, a firm grip but not painfully so.

"I'd better get going to the Forest Kitchen, have a great day. See you at the gate at five." Charlie gave him a grin and a wink and was gone. Nate swallowed and looked at Lennon.

Lennon had long brown hair pulled back in a ponytail and a friendly smile.

"Wow," said Lennon. "I can see why they cast you as Prince Valor."

"Oh, um... Thanks." Nate could feel warmth in his cheeks.

"Come on, let's get to the dressing rooms."

It was almost eerie walking through the park when it was deserted. The only people Nate saw were janitors, food and drink staff like Charlie and people like Lennon who were official Park Helpers – the name the Fairyland Corporation gave to the people who hosted events, greeted guests and accompanied all the characters in costume. Nate had initially applied for one of those jobs, but the interviewer had taken his photo and recommended him for character auditions instead.

"My pronouns are they and them, I'm non-binary. What are yours?"

"He and him," Nate said. "That's cool that you can be out about it here. You kind of hear stories about the park being pretty old fashioned."

"It's not as bad as the rumors make out," Lennon waved at a

security guard, who eyed Nate but didn't interrupt. "Like, sure, maybe when it first opened no one could've been gay or trans or whatever, but there was a big Human Resources overhaul a decade ago. The managers are cool now. They have to be, or else they could be up for a discrimination lawsuit."

"That's awesome." Nate instantly felt some of his nervousness fade away. He wasn't sure if he'd have to be in the closet while he worked here, something he hadn't done for years.

"Because it's your first day, you won't be Prince Valor right out of the box. So if you're nervous about that, you can relax."

Nate breathed out, feeling his shoulders slump and a few of the butterflies in his stomach evaporate. The idea that he'd be thrown in the deep end and be a subpar Prince Valor was horrible. He hated the thought of kids coming to see the character and getting some tongue-tied, nervous newbie.

"You'll have to do costume fittings and training sessions with one of the other princes, and then a trial run before you go out into the park. I'll introduce you to the people you'll be working closest with. You'll always be shifted on with the same Princess Patience, and you'll often be working with the same Prince Justice and Princess Honesty, too." Lennon rattled off as they led him through the park. Nate tried not to get distracted by looking at the eerily empty streets.

"Got it," Nate said.

"Rapport between cast members is how we build the Fairyland magic – the visitors can see the honesty in your connection. Not Princess Honesty, the actual honesty."

Nate laughed. "That makes sense."

"You got the contract with all the rules and stuff in it, right?"

"Yeah," Nate said. He had to do his best to make a good impression on the other staff working as characters. He felt out of his depth with the Fairyland stuff, but at least he knew how to make friends.

"I'll have to go over it again with you verbally, then we take a copy of the contract and file it. But generally <u>the only really big rule you have to stick to is to never break character. They don't care if you swear or fart or go around with no shirt on behind the scenes, but when you're out here as Prince Valor? You *are* Prince Valor. You speak politely, you're respectful and courteous, and you have no bodily functions. If you need to burp? You swallow it.</u> Got it?"

"I got it." Nate chuckled. None of this was a surprise. <u>The princes and princesses of Fairyland were paragons. Too nice to be real.</u> They were named after virtues after all, and the park took that very seriously.

"And about Princess Patience," Lennon continued as they led him through the Enchanted Forest and down the side of the Haunted Tree ride. They opened a gate that said 'staff only', and Nate felt a little thrill. Here was a part of the park he'd never been allowed access to before.

"You'll have to look after her. You can very low-key flirt with the visitors, but only the women. And keep it so squeaky-clean they can't tell if you're actually flirting or just being a charming prince."

"Do the visitors ever flirt with the characters?" Nate asked.

"Oh stars, yes, they're terrible! They will hold onto you for photos, and their hands will wander. They'll touch your butt if they think they can get away with it. They'll kiss your cheek – *do not kiss them back*. Tell them your heart belongs to Princess Patience, and they'll swoon. Did you get that? Play up your devotion. Offer Patience your arm any time you're walking somewhere together. Being madly in love with her will protect you from them."

Nate didn't realize that he had been holding his breath through that whole speech. He breathed out noisily. He'd never imagined the chaste prince would be fending off sexual harassment, but in a way it also made sense. People were obsessed with this park, with these characters. Nate was practically one of them. Sure, he'd read (and even written) some Prince and Princess fanfiction, but he'd always thought of that as separate to the actual people who worked in the park.

"If they get too handsy or actually are groping you, let me know. You can wave or beckon me," Lennon said. "We can get security and toss people out of the park. We want you to be safe, so don't be shy about telling me."

"Thanks," Nate said. He felt a little better.

Lennon slowed as they reached a building butting up against the side of the Haunted Tree ride. The building's wall was painted the same green as the trees planted around it. There were a couple of windows and a blank door with nothing but an electronic lock on it. Lennon swiped their staff ID over it and the door opened.

"Does my staff ID do that, too?" Nate asked.

"Mm-hmm, they have digital tags," Lennon said. They held the door open and gestured for him to enter.

Inside was a long room with some snack and drink vending machines against the wall. There was a large window behind the machines, revealing a view of the backlot. There were a few chairs along the long wall, a table with a coffee machine on it, two doors with crowns painted on them. At the other end there was another door with the word 'Office' painted on it.

"We call this room the airlock," Lennon said.

A man wearing a polo shirt that read Security on the back was the only person inside. He looked like he'd been in the military, from his short tidy hair and the upright posture. He turned from the coffee machine and looked them both over.

"Hey, Cody, this is Nathaniel, he's our new Prince Valor."

Nate held a hand out to Cody. "You can call me Nate," he said. Cody took his hand firmly and shook it. The strength in that handshake matched with Nate's impression of him as ex-military.

Cody's shoulders seemed to suggest he could scoop Nate up and carry him princess style with little effort. He had piercing eyes, but his smile changed his face from intimidating to friendly.

Even so, he was still somewhat terrifying. He had an aura about him, the aura of 'could kick your ass before you raised your fists.'

"Welcome aboard. Don't let Dash put you off, he got up on the wrong side of the castle today."

Nate was relieved when Cody let go of his hand. He'd started to feel his finger bones grinding together. He tried to shake his fingers out subtly.

"Who's Dash?"

Lennon rolled their eyes and huffed out their breath. "You'll be working with him."

Lennon led Nate to one of the doors with a little crown painted on it. Inside was a green-room with rows of lockers, racks of costumes, private changing stalls and a row of makeup stations. The stations were like something out of a theatre, chairs at counters with little drawers and mirrors circled with light bulbs.

"This… is Dashiel," Lennon said. They led Nate to the most gorgeous man he'd ever seen. He'd been sitting at a station, but he stood and walked over at Lennon's words. He was tall, his eyes blazing blue, with a thick crown of golden blond hair, waved to perfection. He wasn't just playing Prince Justice. He *was* Prince Justice. His cheekbones could cut glass, and his jawline was strong but not too big. He could have stepped directly out of the pages of the Princess Honesty book.

"You're… perfect," Nate breathed. His mouth had gone dry.

"What was that?" Dashiel had a distinct air of irritation about him, very unlike the warm manner Prince Justice had in the cartoons.

"Dash, this is Nate," Lennon said quickly. They shot Nate a knowing smile and faintly shook their head.

"I'm the new Prince Valor," he said. He held his hand out, and Dashiel glanced down at it.

Nate's heart dropped. He hadn't even realized his heart had been soaring, but the thrill of meeting the living embodiment of

Prince Justice would do that to him, he guessed. But he wasn't acting like he'd expect Prince Justice to act.

"I'm, um, pleased to meet you?' Nate's hand was still sticking out, so he ran it through his hair.

"Is he going to be out there today?" Dashiel ignored Nate, speaking straight to Lennon.

"Yes, as a handler," Lennon said. "Learning the ropes. He'll need some training, and Wardrobe needs time to get his costume fitted. Today he's shadowing and signing his basic human rights away."

Lennon gave Nate a friendly wink.

Dashiel raised an eyebrow and looked Nate up and down. <u>It felt like a stringent evaluation – not just of his body and looks, but of his personal integrity. And somehow, he already felt he was failing.</u>

"So, this is the guy's changing room," Lennon said, breaking the silence. "The women, the princesses mostly, get ready next door." Lennon pointed at the wall.

"The other room with the crown on the door," Nate said.

"Right. And obviously, no going in there unless you're invited. No peeking at the girls getting changed, don't be gross."

Nate nodded and felt his gaze drawn from Lennon's face to Dashiel.

Dashiel had moved back to the chair he'd been sitting on when they walked in. The station he sat at had a couple of photos arranged neatly around the outside of it, and there were some cosmetics in careful order in front of him. As he picked up a cup of coffee, he looked over and Nate quickly looked away again.

Lennon cleared his throat. "I'm sure you saw this in your pack, and it should go without saying, but there's a 'not in the park' rule."

"Uhm, not in the park?" Nate asked.

<u>"Don't screw the crew, tickle the talent, waltz with your workmates. Don't date or fool around with anyone who works</u>

10

<u>here.</u> It's too risky, and if anyone found out, it could mean termination. Like, no more job." Lennon looked between Nate and Dashiel.

Nate's stomach twisted unexpectedly.

From the cool way in which Dashiel was acting, it wasn't as if he had any hope of action. But Nate's heart or some other parts of him had gotten their hopes up from the moment they'd seen him.

"Yeah, okay, that... umm, that makes sense," he said. He felt like he'd said the same few words of agreement all morning, over and over to Lennon.

"<u>So, even though Ariana is basically a supermodel, no falling in love with her.</u> It's just play acting, got it? No real emotions," Lennon said.

"<u>There's no danger of that,</u>" Nate said, confidently, making a joke of it. "<u>Because I'm really gay. Like, so gay.</u>"

From his seat nearby, Dashiel coughed into his coffee and had to dab himself dry with a paper towel.

Lennon raised their eyebrows and stifled a smile by biting their lip.

"<u>Well that makes it easier for both of you, I guess. And Dash is impossible to work with, so no danger of falling in love there.</u>"
They raised their voice for this last bit and Dashiel coughed again.

"Do you mind? I'm trying to prepare," Dashiel said. "So if you're done outing me to the newbie."

Nate did a double take. *Dashiel was gay too? Fuck.*

"Yeah, no danger at all," Nate said, quickly. He felt lightheaded, but that was probably just from the excitement of the day.

"Come on." Lennon took Nate to the rack of costumes and pulled out a coat hanger with something Nate recognized instantly. Prince Valor's signature outfit. "How about we do the fun stuff and get you properly fitted before we do the paperwork? Once you've had the costume on, I know you won't do a runner."

"Oh, there's no chance of that," Nate said.

11

"Even after an encounter with Dash?" Lennon raised an eyebrow. "You must *really* want this job."

"I really do." He reached out to touch the soft brocade fabric of the tunic. The detailing was incredible, it took his breath away.

Prince Valor's costume was gorgeous. Fitted soft grey pants, a white shirt and a shiny brocade vest over the top. Nate was in love.

"Oh, you have to meet the geniuses in Wardrobe," Lennon said. They took him out the back door of the changing room, across a little stretch of backlot to a huge building stuffed with fabric, costumes, sewing machines and people.

He hoped his disastrous first meeting with Dashiel wasn't going to repeat itself with the Wardrobe crew. He tried to pull himself together so he could make a good impression. What was he going to look like in that gorgeous costume? He could hardly wait to find out.

2 / DASH

Dash peered into the mirror, trying to decide if he needed another layer of foundation. The sun was dazzling but the makeup had a good sunscreen in it. You couldn't be too careful after all – no one wanted to see a sunburned prince.

New-guy Nate and Lennon had just left, and with their exit, the awkward feelings that had stifled all the air in the room had gone too. He looked at himself in the mirror and shook his head. It was one hundred percent not going to happen.

You will not get a crush on the new Prince Valor. No way. Absolutely out of the question. Not for all the hummus in California. Dash stared himself down in the mirror.

Besides, he didn't get crushes. He had one-night stands and even those were rare enough. He couldn't risk dating. What if someone leaked photos of him kissing a guy and linked him to Prince Justice? It was okay if the staff knew he was gay, but if someone put photos of Justice online, kissing men? Well, there were plenty of parents who'd suddenly stop coming to Fairyland, that was for sure.

Not to mention that dating would distract him from the job. He'd tried to date early on, soon after he'd first become Prince Justice, but it was a disaster. His boyfriend wanted him to spend almost all his time with him, and he didn't sleep well with someone else in his bed, and then he wasn't as good on the job.

And nothing was worth losing this job. Even the thought of it set his heart racing and he had a wave of concern. *What can I do better? How can I keep this job?*

He'd worked too hard for too long to get this role, and no one was going to take it away from him now. Not if he had any say in the matter.

Dash had started in the Fairyland Summer Camp intern program. He'd stayed squeaky clean through the three-month internship. While his fellow interns were smoking, drinking or sneaking out to go to clubs, he'd had a rigorous routine: review what he'd learned that day, record his reflections in a journal and in bed by nine thirty. Lights out at ten and a full night's sleep. He'd wake up early each day so he could be prompt and reliable for each day's work.

The work hadn't been glamorous, but he'd put effort into it. Whether it was litter patrol around the park, ticket booth duty or cleaning the bathrooms, he did it to the best of his ability. He hadn't complained, he'd just got through it. He'd kept his goal in mind.

He lived and breathed Fairyland and dreamed of being a prince, someday.

Once the internship was finished, his manager called him into the office. They said he'd been a good, hard worker and he was offered a job as a park greeter. He'd spent long days standing in one spot and saying *good morning, good afternoon* and *good evening* a hundred times an hour. It had been challenging, but he'd stayed on his feet even when they ached and burned in the sun. He'd stayed cheerful, and he gave every visitor a winning smile. He'd worked hard at it, and again dedication was noticed.

His supervisor got him a promotion to tour guide, and he worked hard to get a high feedback rating from the visitors on his tours. The people he took on tours in those days were rich visitors who had paid a hefty fee to have a private guide. The tour included skipping queues and a catered lunch. Dash had taken them to some approved behind the scenes spots and regaled them with stories about the park's early days, and the genius of Dracine Jones.

His reviews and ratings were soon all nines and tens out of ten. Soon enough, people started to return and ask for him specifically.

After he had turned twenty-four and worked out religiously for a year, he auditioned for a character role. Prince Justice.

He hadn't got it on his first audition. They'd cast someone with more muscles than him. So he'd continued his workouts, pushing himself to lift more weights each day, even if his day had been exhausting. He stayed positive even on the days when he'd had to escort a large, whiny family through the drizzling rain, tried to get them excited about trivia. He had never had to pretend enthusiasm when he told the bored, tired tourists the importance of the values and virtues personified by the characters in the stories and how it could inspire people to change their lives, or the world.

Dash shook his head and refocused. He always got distracted when he thought of Dracine Jones and her big dream.

The man who had got the Justice role after Dash's first audition only lasted ten months before quitting. By then, Dash had been ready. He'd aced the next audition and gotten the part. He'd been Prince Justice for almost three years now, and he was well aware that once he passed thirty they'd start looking for a younger man. But for now, he was determined to enjoy his golden years – and he had at least three more to go.

He scowled at himself in the mirror. In waltzed Nate, who hadn't been through the intern program. Dash knew he hadn't, because he'd never seen him working as a greeter or around the park or as a janitor.

Being Prince Justice was the best thing he'd ever achieved. He loved everything about the job. He loved meeting little kids, especially the make a wish ones. He loved seeing the way their eyes lit up when he met with them. The smiles in the photos they took together.

He loved meeting the older fans too; the ones who came in every week, who showed him new items in the Justice collections or wanted new and interesting selfies with him. The ones who asked him to flex his bicep or play around with poses.

Whenever he had an interaction like that, he knew he'd made someone's day better. Maybe even their lives. <u>He loved that he was making the world a little more magical.</u> He always slept better on those nights, satisfied and happy.

That was what drove him, and that was why he took his job seriously. That was why he couldn't mess it up for some cute guy. And yeah, Nate was cute. Those eyes - so bright. And his shy little 'please like me' smile.

He did look like the cartoon prince, and Dash knew if he was good in the role, he'd make Valor just as popular as Justice. The last Valor hadn't been nearly as good as Dash was, no threat at all.

<u>Maybe between them and the princesses they could do something really amazing.</u> Maybe even show the managers and decision-makers that it was time for a live-action version of the princess stories, starring himself and the others.

He rolled his eyes at himself. Now he was just getting silly. There was no talk about new movies – he was letting his imagination run away with him.

He checked himself in the mirror again and smiled. *Perfect.*

He stood up, ensuring the costume was perfectly in place and went to the airlock to wait for the first encounter.

As he stepped out, Neve and Greer were emerging from the women's changing room. Greer played Princess Honesty and Neve was her handler. He'd always thought 'handler' was a weird term, but they didn't have a better one. Chaperone? Nah, that was even worse.

"Morning, Dash," Greer said, giving him a finger wave. He moved in for a quick hello hug. Greer was his closest friend in the park. It made sense that they were that close, given they were almost always working together.

"We've got a new Valor," he said, as he let her go.

"I heard!" Greer replied. She flicked the long auburn locks of her Princess Honesty wig back over her shoulder. "Right off the street too."

"Right off the street?" Dash asked.

"First audition," Greer said. He got the idea this irked her as much as it did him.

"Well, he does know someone in food services," Neve said. "So he was referred. Have you seen him? He looks so—"

"—Right for the part," Dash cut in. He'd been sure she'd say handsome and he didn't want to hear that.

"Ari will be so glad about not going solo anymore," Greer said. She gave Dash a sharp look for interrupting Neve.

"There's talk of changing up the parade, maybe adding some more floats or highlighting more characters," Neve said. She eyed Dash. She had to know this was big news, and yet she was saying it like it was nothing.

"You mean increasing certain character's roles?" Greer said.

"Yeah, that's the rumor. I think it means a lot of people will be watching the new Prince Valor. And you two, over the next couple of weeks. I mean, it is just a rumor though."

"But... Nate's never done a job like this before," Dash said, surprised.

The idea that there was a chance of a promotion or some kind of improved role in the parade was the best news he'd heard in a while. It meant more time that Prince Justice could be winning over fans, more attention from the higher ups. But he couldn't enjoy it, because it wasn't just on offer to him. Apparently a newbie with no experience would also be up for consideration? It was laughable!

Dash scoffed. "He probably thinks it's an easy job, too – just standing around and waving to the crowds. My money's on him not lasting more than a week."

"Dash–" Neve warned, but Dash wasn't done making his point.

"I mean it," He continued, gesturing with one hand. "This is a tough job, and he's probably going to burn out or run away like the last guy did. I mean, he's *clearly* got no idea what he's doing and, honestly? I hope he fails sooner rather than later. For all of our sakes. I hate when these things drag out."

Dash heard someone clearing their throat behind him and turned to see Lennon and Nate standing in the doorway to the prince's changing room.

Dash startled and looked down, folding his arms to cover his reaction. He really hadn't meant to be overheard. But it was too late now. He mostly meant what he'd said, hadn't he? And if there was going to be any extra roles for princes, it should go to him. He'd earned it.

"If you're quite done," Lennon said. "Nate's going to act as a handler today. Give him some time to learn the schedule. He'll mostly be following me around."

"Oh, so you'll be with us all day? Excellent!" Greer floated forward in full Princess Honesty mode. All charm, she shook his hand. He smiled back at her, looking a little dazed.

Dash was on fire with shame. The idea that he'd been badmouthing Nate on his first day, and he'd overheard it. It was so unchivalrous, and although he knew Justice was a part, he generally tried to be noble like him if he could. Besides, he was gazing at Greer as if she were a cartoon come to life, and that was pretty damn adorable.

"Yes, I'm Nathaniel. Nate," he said. "Pleased to meet you."

"In civvies, I'm Greer," she said. "But I'm Princess Honesty the rest of the time. You, me, Dash and Ari will have shifts together –

as long as you get approved, that is. Almost like double dates!" She giggled and Dash tried not to visibly bristle.

She was trying to smooth things over, but she was also clearly enjoying that Dash had been caught out like he was.

"Come on then," Neve said. She shot a quelling glare at Dash. "It's almost time for your appearance at the Reflecting Lake."

Dash cleared his throat out of habit. Nate looked over, as if he expected him to say something. Dash met caught the look of hurt in his eyes before he quickly looked away.

Better he stays away from me than has an awkward crush, Dash thought to himself. He adjusted his costume one more time and cleared his throat. He had to get back into the right frame of mind for Justice, but he was feeling too many things. He had to get on top of that, and fast.

3 / NATE

NATE PULLED ON THE BLUE 'HANDLERS AND HOSTS' POLO SHIRT.

"Wear this," Lennon said, handing him a Fairyland branded sunhat. "It's hot out there. Enjoy the shade while you can, my friend."

They offered him an earpiece next and he put it on. "Follow my lead, and Neve's. I'll go first and clear the way. Neve will walk with Dash and Greer and you follow. They'll be fully in character from the moment we step outside. You're there so no one tries to grab them or stop them for a photo."

"I thought it was okay to take photos of them?" Nate asked.

"Only in approved areas," Lennon said. "In the photo nook at the Reflecting Lake, by the castle or in the rose garden. Obviously, we can't stop people taking photos of them walking past, but the posed stuff all happens in the approved zones only. You know where those places are?"

Nate nodded. "Yeah, I've been to the park a lot," He patted his pants and huffed his breath out. Lennon reached over and pulled his staff ID lanyard out of his shirt.

"Nervous? Don't be. This is the easy part. Being the prince will be the hard stuff."

"Dashiel totally hates me, doesn't he?" Nate said, his voice broke making him sound insecure. He hadn't meant to say that. He'd meant to thank them, or say he was ready, or... something. Literally anything other than that.

Lennon shrugged and gave him a half smile. "Don't take it personally. Dash dislikes everyone to start with. But he is spectacularly good at being Prince Justice. You'll believe he loves everyone he meets. In real life, he's not quite so gregarious. He spends a lot of time at the gym, and eating really healthy. You know, no carbs, it affects his mood, makes him a little cranky, but he's a good guy."

Nate was comforted by Lennon's words. It seemed like they'd just described half the guys he'd dated back in San Francisco before he moved out here.

"You've got this," Lennon took hold of his shoulders and gave him a reassuring squeeze. "Your job is to fade into the background and make things easier. Do whatever you can to elevate the guest's experience and spread a little Fairyland magic. We'll be out there for about an hour with Neve, Dash, and Greer. Then we'll come back here to rest and hydrate before the parade."

"Wait... I'll be in the parade?" His heart started racing again. All those people watching him, potentially judging...

"Yep! Today think of yourself as a bodyguard to Princess Honesty and Prince Justice."

He breathed a little easier then. The idea of being a royal bodyguard was fun, even if the guy playing the prince was an entitled asshole.

"Here's hoping for an uneventful day, then," Dashiel said from behind him.

"Now Dash, be nice to the newbie," Greer warned. Nate turned back to face them. She stepped up beside Dashiel, now with a twinkling tiara sitting on top of her perfectly coiffed wig, her dress was a long ball gown in a stunning mid purple color. She seemed to have been airbrushed with pixie dust.

Dashiel, on the other hand, looked like he'd stepped right out of one of Nate's favorite fanfics.

I think I dreamed he was rescuing me and then we made out once, Nate thought.

Dashiel was resplendent in full Prince Justice regalia. A sword strapped to his hip, a bright red and gold tabard belted over his loose, pristine white shirt and fitted black pants and boots. His hair and teeth practically gleamed.

Nate forgot how to breathe, he just stared at Dashiel in wonder. He truly was Prince Justice, every inch of him. If only he had the same kind nature the prince had in the movies, Nate thought.

Lennon listened to their earpiece for a moment and signaled for Nate to turn on his own. "We've got the all clear. Gates have been open for an hour, time to head out."

"Try and keep up," Dashiel said. He intentionally brushed Nate's shoulder as he followed Neve. Greer rested her hand lightly on Dashiel's proffered forearm.

Nate set his jaw. Dashiel might be handsome – heck, he might even be the most handsome man Nate had ever seen – but he was absolutely not going to get the satisfaction of seeing Nate fail.

Nope. Nate had made up his mind. He was going to be the best damn handler, and later, the best damn Prince Valor Fairyland had ever seen.

4 / NATE

The park wasn't too busy yet. But even still, as soon as Dashiel lead Greer through the gate and into the park proper, they got attention. Neve led them at a quick pace, smiling wide with the signature Fairytale beam. Dashiel and Greer followed, almost seeming to float. Nate couldn't help but be impressed.

Dashiel's walk had changed: he was striding but in a smooth way. Purposeful, military but graceful. Greer had become Princess Honesty for real, her arm resting lightly on Dashiel's arm, the other at her side but not hanging limp. It was held like a ballet dancer's, palm facing down and her fingers held elegantly up a little.

They smiled at the visitors they passed, and Nate saw how they paid attention as he hurried behind them. Dashiel and Greer made eye contact with the children and waved back at them. Greer greeted guests almost constantly.

Nate smiled as well, hoping it was bright enough to count as Fairyland standard. He noticed from his position at the end of the retinue that people were beginning to follow them. Not in a creepy way, just in a 'yay look there's Princess Honesty!' way.

Neve led them to an arch beside the Reflecting Lake with a

cobblestone path leading up on one side, a topiary replica of the castle on the other.

It was picturesque.

Dashiel spun Greer around elegantly and she giggled musically. Neve moved to the left-hand side of the arch and Lennon gestured for Nate to take the right. Lennon stayed at the entrance to the arch and escorted the first guest from the rapidly forming line.

A Hispanic woman with two children who were bouncing and squealing with excitement were first up.

A man in the same polo that Nate, Neve, and Lennon were all wearing appeared with a fancy digital camera.

"Simon! There you are. Perfect timing." Lennon looked relieved as Simon took up a position several feet back from the archway and started snapping photos of the mom and her children with the prince and princess.

In the time it took for the first group to get photos taken with the prince and princess, the queue was about fifty people long.

Neve gestured for the next person in the queue to move forward and Nate did the same for the next in line when the time came. Simon the photographer was a natural, coaxing kids to look his way and getting smiles out of everyone. He also seemed to be taking candid photos when they first met the characters, which Nate thought would probably be the best ones. He would even take the visitor's phones if they asked and take a few with those too.

Nate noticed a beaming parent stay back from the meet and greet just to take photos of her kids with the characters. When that happened, Nate moved in.

The woman was juggling her camera, her phone and a couple of bags of merchandise.

"Hey, how about I take some photos with all of you in there?" Nate said.

She looked at him uncomprehending for a moment and he

smiled, unsure if he needed to repeat himself. Then his words seemed to filter through and she nodded.

"That would be wonderful, if you could!"

"Absolutely," Nate said. "You can leave the bag here with me too." She handed her camera over and spent a couple of seconds explaining how to take photos with it, and left her shopping bags at his feet. He took a number of photos, trying to frame them as nicely as he could.

As the group broke up to move on and he was handing the camera and bags back to the lady Simon gave him a thumbs up and a smile.

"Good work," Neve said as he moved back into his position.

The line moved quickly and Nate lost track of time. Dashiel and Greer spent a few minutes with each visitor, chatting and asking questions, or answering them. But it soon became clear to Nate that it was kind of exhausting being this friendly all the time. Dashiel and Greer didn't look tired at all though, and they never once broke character. Nate found himself admiring the easy chemistry they had with each other, and the way they could read the visitors.

Then, one group of younger women had wanted to fawn over Prince Justice.

"We have to have a photo with just the Prince!" One of them exclaimed.

Greer had moved a little to the side, smiling still, and spoke to Neve about something while she waited for them to finish. She made it so easy for the women to have photos with just the prince, and it wasn't awkward at all.

When one little boy only had eyes for Princess Honesty, Dashiel had moved behind the two of them and watched over them with a protective air, not saying anything. Greer had knelt down, spreading the skirts of her dress, and looked the little boy in the eyes as they talked quietly. It was a real performance, but a mindful one. Nate made a lot of mental notes as he watched them. They were exceptionally good at this, putting in a lot of effort to make everyone feel special, and Nate felt both excited and nervous. There was no doubt in his mind that it was going to be a lot of hard work, and he was nervous he wouldn't be able to pull it off the same way Greer and Dashiel could. But the challenge was exciting as well.

Dashiel helped Greer to her feet with ridiculous grace once the little boy skipped away, and for a second there was quiet moment when no new guests came forward.

There must be a gap in the queue, Nate thought.

He frowned. Wait, why was there a gap in the queue? The line had still been endless the last time Nate had noticed it. He tore his attention away from the prince and princess to see the next person in line was a little girl, probably four or five years old. She wore a fluffy kid's version of Princess Honesty's dress and she was trying to hide behind the legs of the man she was with. Nate guessed he was her father from the matching straight black hair.

"Go on, honey," the man was saying. "You've been waiting for this." He sighed and looked at Nate. "She's been so excited to meet her. All week it's been Princess Honesty this, Princess Honesty that. Now she's gone shy."

"It's no problem," Nate said. He smiled warmly and approached the two of them, trying his best to have open, welcoming body language.

Behind the father and her little girl, Lennon was dealing with the next people in line. Neve was helping Greer spread out the skirts of her dress. *It's up to me*, he thought, nervously.

Nate knew exactly how this kid felt. If he'd had a sturdy pair of legs to hide behind this morning, he might have. He went down to one knee so he wouldn't be too big and scary to the little girl. He gave her a reassuring smile.

"Hey there, I'm Nate," he said. He tried to catch her eye but only one of them was visible. Half her face was hidden behind her father's pant leg. She looked back with one dark brown eye. "Is this your first time meeting the prince and princess?" He asked, keeping his voice on the quieter side.

She eyed him for a moment, uncertain, and then nodded.

"Well, guess what?" he said. "It's my first day working at Fairyland today. So I met them for the first time today, too."

Her little fist relaxed and let go of her father's pant leg and she moved out from behind him a little. Nate could see her whole face now, and her attention was riveted on him. Her head tilted to the side, and he read the question in it.

"Yeah, and I was a bit scared to meet them, too. Princess Honesty is so elegant and so beautiful, and Prince Justice? Well, he's brave and noble. But guess what? They're really nice, too, and I know they'd like to meet you. They've been very kind to me, and I'm not dressed anywhere near as fancy as you are."

The girl smiled and moved towards him, her hands moving to fluff her skirts a little.

"Do you like my dress?" she asked.

"I love it. It's so beautiful," Nate said. "What's your name, sweetheart?"

"Minako," the little girl said.

"That's a great name. I bet Princess Honesty will like it too. Shall we go and show her your dress?" Nate asked.

Minako looked up at her father, who nodded his head. Then she grabbed Nate's hand, her tiny fingers closing tight around his. Much stronger than he'd anticipated, actually.

"Is it okay?" Nate asked the father.

"Please, it would mean the world to her." He pulled out his phone, getting ready for a photo.

Nate stood up and led Minako over to Dashiel and Greer, who were now ready and waiting.

"Princess Honesty, Prince Justice, may I present the Lady Minako?" Nate said, as grandly as he could. He brought Minako forward and guided her in front of him. She hesitated, squeezing his hand hard. How could such a tiny hand have such a fierce grip? He tried not to wince.

Greer smiled and bent forward, her hands on the front of her own skirt, making herself a little smaller.

"I'm so pleased to meet you, Lady Minako. Your dress is beautiful!"

Minako made a tiny squeaky noise and let go of Nate's hand to throw her arms around Greer's neck. Greer, who had obviously had this happen before, caught the little girl and rocked back on her heel a tiny bit so she didn't fall over.

Nate moved back into his position at the side of the arch, his smile now genuinely large, not forced. He'd done good, he knew it, he'd tapped into the Fairyland magic and now he felt on a high from it. The nervous butterflies had vanished from his stomach.

Minako's father was snapping photo after photo, Simon alongside him doing the same thing. Minako's father looked over at Nate and mouthed the words 'thank you'. Nate shook his head, like it was nothing, but he knew he was still beaming. He mouthed 'you're welcome' back.

Minako tugged on Greer's sleeve - she was still crouched at her level - and whispered something in her ear. "Of course." She turned her head to look at Dashiel. "Prince Justice, the Lady Minako would like a photo with you, if that's all right."

Dashiel smiled and bowed with a flourish.

"It would be an honor, my lady." He went to one knee and put his arm around Minako's shoulders. She beamed, leaning against him and waving at the cameras.

Minako kissed Dashiel's cheek and said goodbye to both of them. Simon pulled a token out of his pocket and handed it to Minako's father.

"Take this, you need those photos," he said.

"Hmm?" Minako's father looked bewildered.

"It's a photo pass coin. Give them that token and they'll give you prints to take home, no charge."

Minako's father beamed. "Thank you so much." For a second, Nate thought he caught a shimmer of glassy tears. His heart thumped happily and seemed to warm his chest. *I did good.* "Thank you. You've made today truly magical." He turned to Nate and squeezed his hand as he shook it. "Thank you, really. Thank you."

"Any time, you're welcome," Nate said. As he waved them off, his shoulders relaxed properly for maybe the first time all day. He'd done it. He'd delivered a little of the Fairyland magic like Lennon had been talking about. He'd succeeded on his first day.

He turned to check that Lennon had the line moving forward to meet Prince Justice and Princess Honesty. When he looked back again, he saw Dashiel watching him.

<u>His face had been the friendly mask of Prince Justice's smile the whole time they'd been out in the park, but for the first time, Nate thought it looked like a sincere smile. His eyes had crinkled up, and his smile seemed softer somehow.</u>

Nate returned the smile, a little uncertain, and Dashiel instantly looked away, focusing on the elderly guests in front of him. Nate's heart fluttered hesitantly and he swallowed.

Had that been real? Or had Nate imagined it? Was it just Dashiel caught up in being Prince Justice, or did they just have a moment?

5 / DASH

As far as meet and greets went, it was medium-level busy, standard for a Monday morning. He imagined Nate had been surprised at how busy it was. Surely on a weekday morning, everyone would be at work or in school, yes? If not that, then running errands or doing chores.

But Fairyland was a special place. There were people who came every week and a handful of people who came almost every day. People with year-long passes, or three-month seasonal passes. People visited the Fairyland grounds in the same way as someone might take a stroll around their local park.

On top of that, there were always tourists and kids skipping school, young parents who wanted to show their babies something magical, or just regular people giving themselves a treat day. Some schools sent kids here on field trips, even.

All of those visitors were important, Dash knew, and all of them deserved a perfectly magical experience.

Dash was outwardly everything Prince Justice should be, but inwardly, his thoughts kept returning to Nate. He tried to let it go, but for some reason he kept thinking about him. How was he finding the queue? How would he cope when the park got really busy? Was he going to mess up and make Dash look bad? It was lucky he was so practiced at being Prince Justice, or he may have come across distracted.

Then Nate surprised him: he got down on one knee and coaxed a shy little girl forward. He was clearly a natural with kids. He knew to get down on her level but left enough space so she didn't feel threatened. He got her name so that Greer could take over from him with no trouble. And then it had turned out it was really him the little girl was shy of.

Dash posed for a photo with her and beamed – but inside he was in turmoil.

If Nate was a natural charmer, then when he put on the costume and became Prince Valor he was going to quickly become a fan favorite.

And maybe rightfully so, a voice in his head chimed in. *He was handsome, sweet, genuine and sensitive. Why shouldn't he succeed?*

Really handsome, Dash thought. But he couldn't let himself notice that too often.

But if Valor became a favorite, what would happen to Justice? Fairyland fans held a lot of sway over how things happened at the park. Social media was hugely important to the people running marketing and events. Just look at what had happened with Good Fairy Gentle when Rosa took over. She'd brought some of her own interpretation and personality to the role, and when word got around that Fairy Gentle was not only beautiful but sassy and mischievous, she'd blown up on social media.

Not Rosa herself, of course. They all had to sign Non-Disclosure Agreements on not talking about life in the park on social media.

Photos of Fairy Gentle were all over Instagram. The Fairyland fan blogs filled up with details on when to see her, reports of her doing cute things and stories of encounters full of magic.

Suddenly Rosa was being asked to do more shifts, more meet and greets and a special appearance at a character-themed lunch in the Forest Kitchen. She got her own float in the parade and a featured photo spot in the Enchanted Forest.

The other fairies: Kindness, Respect, Mischief, Giggle and the twin fairies Song and Dance, faded into the background of park life. Not that they weren't still given meet and greets, but it was Gentle who became the star.

There were already a lot of princes in the Fairyland stories, Dash thought uncomfortably. Prince Magnificence and Prince Diligence were already very popular. They weren't a threat though, as the park split their shifts. If Dash and whoever was Valor were on in the morning, Magnificence and Diligence were on in the evening and vice versa.

Nate was a different story. Nate could pose a real threat to the success Dash was enjoying as Prince Justice. In his role as Prince Justice, he wasn't a runaway fan favorite the way Fairy Gentle was, but he was popular. He had his fans.

But Nate as Prince Valor? He had the potential to get to Rosa's level of popularity if that moment was anything to go by. The thought made his stomach clench up and he had to swallow down some panic.

"Are you alright?" Greer asked in an almost silent whisper as they embraced for a photo.

"Sure, yeah, I am," he replied at the same volume.

"You're a thousand miles away," she said. They let each other go and waved off the guests who had been posing with them. As they greeted the next people in line, Dash shifted his weight onto one foot, paying attention to the feel of physical pressure to distract himself. He had to focus.

Already the new guy was putting him off his game, and Nate wasn't even in the prince costume yet. His heart and mind raced and he had to force himself to breathe slowly and evenly.

But Nate hadn't earned it yet, and hopefully Dash had a few more weeks before he had to consider Nate as competition for real.

He's going to look so freaking gorgeous in that costume. The colors in it would really make his eyes pop, he thought, picturing it. He banished the unbidden image away and curled his fist, digging his nails hard into his palm.

Focus, he reminded himself. It was almost time for a break, and if Greer had noticed he was distracted, it was only a matter of time before Neve or Lennon caught on, and he couldn't have that.

6 / NATE

THERE WAS AN HOUR OF REST TIME BEFORE THE MUSTER FOR THE parade. Nate spent it getting to know Ariana, who was going to be the Princess Patience to his Prince Valor.

The princess's changing room was almost a mirror image of the prince's one, except it was larger, with more changing stalls, and the mirrors on their makeup stations had more lights around them. Nate wondered why – surely everyone benefited from having more lights around the mirrors? He shifted from foot to foot, looking inside.

The racks of costumes were bigger, too. The dresses had a lot more volume, so they needed more space than the prince outfits on the men's side.

Technically, he shouldn't be in this dressing room but Ariana had invited him in.

"Are you sure it's okay?" he'd asked, peering around the door. Ariana had waved her hand dismissively.

"Please, we're all adults here, aren't we?"

When he'd hesitated further, Greer had tugged on his hand and pulled him in. "Those rules are only really important if a big boss is around, or if someone's getting up to something naughty."

"And, I'm gay so there won't be any chance of naughtiness," Nate said, allowing himself to be pulled into the room.

"As if I'd let you try anyway," Ariana said lightly, then giggled.

Greer had set aside her auburn Princess Honesty wig and was massaging her hands through her natural blonde hair. There was no one else in the room, but he understood from what Lennon had said that people came and went throughout the day.

Ariana led him to her station, which was decorated with cards and notes from fans. Judging from the handwriting, they were mostly from children.

"So, you literally walked straight into the prince role?" Ariana asked. She pushed a half full box of caramel popcorn to him and then leaned towards her mirror, finishing off her makeup for the parade.

Nate helped himself to the popcorn. He had liked Ariana right away, which was a relief. He didn't know if he could do this job if she'd reacted to him the way Dashiel had.

"I mean, kind of? I'd just been interviewing for a front entrance greeter role and they got all excited and asked me to audition. I wasn't going to say no, I love Prince Valor."

"The last guy did kind of leave abruptly," Ariana said. "Usually people give notice, but he just took off one day."

"Wow... Why would anyone do that?" Nate asked. Although Ariana shrugged, he got the feeling she knew what had happened there.

"Beats me, some people are just assholes."

Nate paused. "So, um, Dashiel," he said. He reached over to take some popcorn out of the box.

"Dashiel," Ariana replied. She caught Nate's eye in the mirror. "What about him?" Her tone was careful. She wasn't going to let anything slip before he did.

"I kind of... I get the feeling he doesn't like me," Nate said. He chewed on some popcorn before continuing. "And not just because he said all that stuff about me not taking the job seriously."

"Are you going to take this job seriously?" She arched a perfect eyebrow and gave him an intense look. He didn't think he could lie to her, even if he wanted to.

"I'm going to do my best every day," he said, meaning it. "I really love this place, and I'm excited about being a part of it."

"You're going to rock it," Greer said. She moved from her own station to sit on the other side of Ariana. "You were amazing with that little girl today."

"You heard what Dash said about me, though," Nate said. He looked down, frowning a little. Those words had hurt. And Dashiel had been in the job long enough to know if someone was going to work out, right? And Nate knew he had so little experience, his learning curve would be steep, and the idea Dashiel would be looking down on him the whole time wasn't exactly comforting. He realised he was bouncing his leg up and down and stopped it.

"Dash is a serious guy and he loves this job. He loves the park. As long as you prove that you're in this for real, he'll come around," Ariana said. She patted Nate's hand. "Have faith in yourself."

"Prove yourself to him," Greer said, nodding in agreement.

Nate could work with that. "Thanks, I think I can do that."

"Okay, but you need to tell us more about you, mystery man." Greer settled on the seat beside Ariana, leaning towards Nate with a wide smile. Ariana nodded in agreement, and they both looked at him expectantly.

"There's not that much to tell. I grew up loving the Fairyland movies. I had the picture books of the stories. Mom bought me the jigsaw puzzles, and the soundtracks to the movies whenever she could find them in thrift stores. We didn't live too close to the park, and we didn't have much money, but my folks scrimped and saved so they could bring us here a couple times."

"Life story, cool. You love Fairyland, we got that. How about the *important* stuff?" Ariana said, half turning in her chair to look at him.

"Important?" Nate realised this was more of an interrogation than small talk, but the girls both seemed friendly enough so he went along with it.

"Have you got a boyfriend?" Greer asked, grinning at him over Ariana's shoulder.

"Oh! No. No one, not for a while," Nate said. He remembered his last boyfriend and frowned some. Ariana and Greer exchanged a suspicious look.

"How'd you get the job then?" Ariana asked.

"My best friend, Charlie. He's in food services. He told me they were hiring and then he referred me. He works at the Enchanted Forest Kitchen."

"And you rocked up looking like the cartoon come to life, and they couldn't resist," Ariana said. She smiled wide, looking him up and down. "Oh, yeah... I think we're going to get on fine."

"Come on, time's a'tickin'." Greer moved back to her mirror and pulled her wig back on. A few more women, mostly dancers from the way they held themselves, filtered into the room to prep for the parade.

"I'd better leave you to it," Nate said. He stood up.

"See you out there. And hey, Nate?" Ariana looked up at him. He paused halfway to the door and half turned, careful to not direct his gaze towards the changing stalls.

"Yeah?"

Ariana smiled. "I just wanted to say I'm looking forward to working with you. Just don't screw it up, okay?"

Nate smiled, nodded and left the room, hoping he looked more confident than he felt.

7 / DASH

THE PARADE ALWAYS STARTED CLOSE TO THE BUILDINGS WHERE THE actors changed into character. Prince Justice and Princess Honesty had a ballroom style float. It had a dance floor with an arched pagoda-style framework over a wide, flat base. It was decorated with vined plastic leaves and sprouting flowers which twined around the support columns. The whole frame had been strung with twinkling fairy lights.

They would alternate waltzing around the floor and standing in the front to wave at the audience, depending on the music throughout the parade. The effect was very pretty, and the float hadn't changed for several years; it was a fixture of the parade. Even if privately Dash was a little sick of it.

Dash helped Greer up the steps and onto the dance floor. They were still backstage in the park but he liked to be courteous to her even when they didn't have an audience. He heard the sound of Ariana laughing and he turned to see her in full Princess Patience regalia, walking with Nate.

Nate met Dash's eye, then said something to Ariana and they both started laughing like two children giggling together.

Dash looked away fast, feeling his cheeks warm. They couldn't be laughing about him, could they? He climbed up onto the float, fuming. If they were going to make fun of him, fine. He could handle it. He'd ignore them and do his job. He wouldn't let it get to him. He realised he was clenching his fist and digging his nails into his palm again. He consciously relaxed his hand.

"Dash, what's up?" Greer asked. She frowned, moving closer to him and adjusting the way his costume jacket sat on his shoulder. It was perfectly fitted, of course, but the epaulets and things sometimes got caught up. For the parade he added a sash over the costume.

"Nothing, thanks," he mumbled. She reached up to fix his hair. He assumed it was more to fuss than there being any hair out of place. He'd already checked it a million times.

"Dash? Breathe. Relax. There's a new guy, whatever. It's going to be fine. You're here with me, your best friend. I'm not going to judge you… but I will tell you when you're being ridiculous."

They knew each other so well it was like she was reading his mind. He sucked in a ragged breath and held it for a moment before huffing it out. He let his shoulders relax.

"There." She squeezed his bicep. "Parade time. You know what to do."

"But… what if he's better than me?" Dash blurted. He looked away from her, mortified. He hadn't meant to say that, it'd slipped out. Like his psyche had pushed it out his mouth, totally bypassing his brain and his better judgment.

Greer chuckled and took his hand. "So *that's* what's got your panties in a twist, is it?"

He looked up at her, feeling a little ill. This was humiliating. A grown man sick to his stomach because someone came along who might be good at a similar job. Was he really this insecure?

"No?" He said in a small voice.

Greer sighed, "You're being ridiculous," she said. But she said it affectionately, like she understood him. "I think you're forgetting that Prince Valor and Prince Justice work alongside each other. Give him a chance. Him being a good Valor won't make you any less impressive as Justice, you know."

Dash took another deep breath and nodded.

They both turned to look at the first float of the parade starting to move. They were fourth in the lineup, and the parade wasn't too big, so it was a good spot. Prince Valor and Princess Patience were walked directly in front of Justice and Honesty's float. For the last two months, while they'd been looking for a new Valor, Patience had walked alone. Once Nate got trained up and his costume was fitted, they'd walk together.

That meant that whatever happened, Nate would be close. Dash had to adjust to the way things were. Try and get along with him as best he could.

He nodded to Greer and they got into the waltz position, her hand on his shoulder and his arm around her waist, their other hands clasped and raised high.

Ariana in her Patience costume started walking. Nate was to the side, acting as a handler. Neve and Lennon were nearby, too, giving the signal to whoever was driving the float today to start it up. The music piped through the loudspeakers got louder as their float started to move and they went through the gates into the park proper.

Park guests with cameras and phones were lining both sides of the road, and Dash made sure to smile. These photos would end up on social media – he had to be picture perfect. It was harder than usual, his mind so preoccupied on his own insecurities.

Dash began leading the spinning, slow waltz they'd done hundreds of times before.

"So um, don't freak out more but I heard something," Greer said, through her teeth, set in the Fairyland standard smile. "That they'll be changing up the parade some."

"I thought it was just a rumor," he said. His stomach started to sink with foreboding. He wished the idea didn't freak him out. But he wanted a better parade float so much, and the idea it could be some other character getting an upgrade and not him was awful. His competitive side was likely to flare up.

"I heard it from Neve, who heard it from her manager," Greer said. "They're thinking of adding a Valor and Patience float." His stomach dropped away.

"You tell me this now? After saying I had nothing to worry about?" He could feel himself tensing just thinking about it.

"What, you think their float is going to be bigger than ours?" Greer teased.

"Maybe," Dash said. He knew even as he said it he was being petty. It wasn't going to make their parade float less pretty. It was a classic image, and one the fans absolutely adored, but then, what if they were all too busy looking at Valor and Patience to notice them any more? He'd worked so hard for so long to be as impressive as he could, he wished the park would reflect that effort back at him a little more. But even as he thought it, he felt guilty. <u>The park had only ever been good to him.</u> The staff had trained, supported and encouraged him and given him this role after all. He should really be grateful.

Greer sighed, shook her head so the curls of her wig tossed prettily. "Just shut up and dance."

8 / NATE

AT THE END OF THE DAY, CHARLIE DROVE NATE HOME. THANKFULLY the traffic out of the staff part of the car park was nothing like the visitor's car park.

"Maybe don't get used to this," Charlie said. Nate, who had been preoccupied with how much his feet ached and draining his water bottle, looked over at him.

"Don't get used to what?"

"Me driving you. Your shifts will be sort of predictable. Mine change around."

"No worries," Nate said. "Thanks for bringing me today and showing me where to go. It made things a lot easier."

"How was your first day?" Charlie asked, looking over at him.

"It was mixed," Nate admitted. "I really like most of the people, but this one guy, Dash? Dashiel? He plays Justice. He's kind of a tool." Nate frowned. He hated to say negative things about people. Generally he thought people were doing the best they could in their circumstances,. But he couldn't get Dashiel's words out of his head.

That Dashiel thought he couldn't do this job.

That he had no idea what this job really meant.

"Well, at least he's a handsome tool," Charlie said, laughing.

Nate rolled his eyes, "Okay, yes, but not the point," he said. "Dashiel thinks I'm useless. That I'm going to mess around and goof off."

"What a jerk," Charlie exclaimed. He thumped his hand on the steering wheel to emphasize his point. Nate felt comforted. He could always rely on Charlie to be on his side.

"It just sucks because I love the idea of this job so much. I want it to be perfect." Nate twisted his lanyard in his hands, then untangled it.

"You want my advice? Just stay out of his way. You have nothing to worry about, you're going to rock it. Besides, the grapevine says if you're impressive enough, they'll put a Valor and Patience float into the parade. But you didn't hear it from me."

That *was* news. Nate looked at Charlie, his heart racing. "For real?"

Charlie nodded.

"Uh huh, Fairyland rumor mill is working overtime. Someone said something about a big animatronic dragon. Sounds badass. Of course, there are lots of rumors which have never come to anything, but I thought you should know, anyway."

Nate settled back. Well that sounded worth dealing with Dashiel for. Just think if there was a new Valor float, and he'd be the Prince Valor who got to appear with it? Fairyland history, and he'd be part of it. His inner seven-year-old was super excited by the thought. He imagined getting photos to send his Mom, she'd be so proud. It would all be worth it…

He'd just have to stay out of Dashiel's way. Keep his head down and do the job the best he could.

9 / NATE

STAYING OUT OF DASHIEL'S WAY WASN'T AS EASY AS NATE HAD anticipated. In fact, it was impossible. They had to get ready in the same changing room. Nate spent two more days as a handler, then Lennon proclaimed him ready for his full-day Valor training. It started off easy enough, with a rewatch of *Princess Patience's Challenge* – the animated movie Valor featured in.

Then Lennon took him to Dashiel.

Nate grabbed Lennon's arm and talked to them in a hushed tone. "Couldn't one of the other guys do it?"

"Who would be better? He's been at this for years, and he knows the prince stuff inside out."

"Okay but–" Nate started. Lennon cut him off.

"Besides, he's brilliant at it. Have you seen the Prince Justice hashtag on Instagram and Twitter?"

"No." Nate sighed. This job had more facets to it than he'd anticipated. He hated feeling like he was behind before he'd even started.

"You should check it out, social media's important in this job." Lennon turned to look over at Neve, who was waving to them. "Just a second." They turned back to Nate. "Face it, you two are stuck with each other. You may as well make the most of it."

Lennon softened a little then and patted Nate on the back. "He's great at this, and you're a natural. Take the guidance and ignore his bad attitude."

Nate nodded and took a breath, steeling himself. "Okay. Thanks, Lennon. I will."

"And hey, you never know, maybe you can charm him into liking you?"

Nate raised an eyebrow. He wasn't sure there was enough charm in the world for that.

Dashiel and Nate spent the rest of the day in one of the green rooms in the back lot.

They both dressed in workout clothes. Dashiel looked over as Nate pulled on his shoes, his eyebrows were drawn down and together and he was frowning. For once, it seemed like they agreed on something.

"We're going to start with posture and gait," Dashiel said. He looked Nate up and down critically. "Well, your posture isn't bad at least, but you have to lift from your core at all times."

"Like this?" Nate straightened his spine and tensed his abs some.

Dashiel looked him over again and frowned.

"Almost, I guess. You can always be better though. Watch me." He walked across the room, demonstrating what Nate had already come to think of as the Justice walk. It did look good.

"It's a very impressive walk, Dash," Nate said, meaning it.

"Call me Dashiel. Only my friends call me Dash," Dashiel said.

Nate prickled. *What a jerk thing to say*, he thought. His spine stiffened and he channeled it into trying the same kind of straight back, flowing walk that Dashiel had demonstrated.

"No. You're too tense. You have to have your back straighter." Dashiel folded his arms and tipped his head to one side.

Nate looked down at his feet and tried to straighten his back more. "Like that?"

Dashiel's planted his hand on the small of Nate's back. "Lift through here."

Nate cleared his throat. Dashiel's hand was warm and firm; he felt heat radiating over his back. He swallowed, tried to ignore that, and the gentle aroma of his cologne. Which was sort of... lemony?

I can do this. He put his shoulders back.

Then Dashiel put his other hand on his stomach. "Engage the muscles here. Tighten them up and *then* walk."

Nate nodded and cleared his throat. His whole body was alert to the two places Dashiel was touching him, and he was at once eager to try but he also wanted to stay put.

"Got it," he said. Dashiel's hands fell away and he tried the walk again, this time consciously engaging his core.

"Better," Dashiel said. Nate turned to see Dashiel looking away, picking up a small towel and dabbing at his face. Nate's shoulders slumped and his abs disengaged.

"But... you weren't even watching."

Dashiel scowled and looked away, his jaw worked for a moment before he replied. "Yes, I was. And you still suck. But now you suck a little less." Dashiel tossed the towel back onto the bench with some force.

"You know what? You could at least be a bit nicer," Nate said. Heat flooded his body. Whatever he'd said to Lennon, he couldn't just ignore this. "I don't actually respond well to the Full Metal Jacket boot camp style of teaching."

"Sorry to disappoint you, but I don't do *nice*," Dashiel spat. "Not to pretty-boy upstarts who waltz their way into my-" Dashiel caught himself. "Into *their* dream jobs without paying any dues or working up to it like the rest of us."

Nate blinked at him, taken aback. Not just by the stutter where Dashiel had talked about his own dream job, but by the paying dues comment.

"Is that what this is about? You're pissed that I didn't start out ten years ago as a janitor?"

Dashiel folded his arms over his chest, his eyebrows shooting up towards his hairline as he took a step back.

I guess I don't look like the kind of guy who'd stand up for himself, Nate thought. He couldn't explain Dashiel moving back like that otherwise.

"N-No, it's not that," Dashiel said. Then he seemed to get a hold of himself and stalked across the room to Nate. He walked with a straight back and a regal grace, perfect, except for the seething anger.

Nate held his ground. How could Dashiel be so infuriating and so attractive at the same time? His heart was thumping hard. Where they about to fight?

"Listen up, newbie." Dashiel prodded Nate in the chest with one finger. "I don't like your attitude. You swan in like... Like I don't even know what. And then everyone just loves you right away? What's your game here?"

"My *game*?" Nate shook his head and backed up a step. His temper had melted away a little in the face of Dashiel's up-close fury.

Nate's back hit the wall of the greenroom as he took another step away from Dashiel. He wasn't sure how they'd got there, and Dashiel was so angry now. He wanted to defuse the situation, if he could. He didn't want a fight. "I – I don't have a game."

"Is this just a job for you?" Dashiel crowded closer to Nate, looming over him. He had at least three inches on him. Nate swallowed. There was that lemony smell again. And his teeth were so white and even.

"No," Nate said. His voice came out a lot breathier than he'd meant.

"Because it's more than a job to me," Dashiel snarled. His breath smelled of mint. "This is my *life*. And if you do anything to screw this up for me, I'm going to make sure you not only lose your job, but you can never show your face here again."

Nate nodded. "Yes. Okay, sir."

Nate closed his eyes and tried to push his way backward through the wall. Why? Why had he said that? Called him sir? Dashiel wasn't his boss. Nate couldn't think straight. His mouth wasn't cooperating. His heart raced.

He opened his eyes again. Dashiel was right there, peering at him, his intense blue eyes seeming to drill into him. Dashiel's lips parted.

Nate looked at those lush lips and felt his own part, heard himself panting all of a sudden. Dashiel was so close. He'd all but pinned Nate to the wall.

"Did... you just call me *sir*?"

Nate inhaled, looking into Dashiel's eyes.

"I want..." Nate breathed, and he trailed off because he couldn't say 'you', could he? Dashiel seemed to be about to punch him, and all Nate wanted was... him?

Then Dashiel kissed him.

It was hot and hard, his tongue flicking out to lick Nate's lower lip.

Nate forgot to breathe. His arms went around Dashiel's neck with no input from his brain. He kissed him back.

What's happening?

Dashiel pushed with his jaw and Nate tipped his head a little to the side. He made a soft noise in his throat, which he hadn't meant to do, but right now his body was doing all kinds of things he didn't mean for it to do.

His mind blurred with conflicting thoughts.

I shouldn't be doing this. But he's so hot. And this kiss is so good. But he literally hates me. But he's kissing me. He's kissing me and he can't stand me. I can't stand him. This kiss is amazing...

Despite the heat of the kiss, Dashiel pulled back, his chest heaving.

"This is ridiculous," Dashiel said, his voice a near growl. Nate nodded, then pulled him in for another kiss.

Dashiel responded by pressing his body against Nate's.

And in an instant, Nate's brain had gone from a flurry of thoughts to just one: *This feels so right.*

None of his exes had ever kissed him like this. Like it was a battle. Like it was a duel to see who'd come out on top.

And now that this duel was happening?

Nate didn't want to win at all.

He wanted to surrender.

10 / DASH

His pulse pounding in his temples, Dash kissed Nate so hard their teeth crashed together. He tried to soften it, tried to pull back, but he was so angry. His frustration made him all the thirstier for more of Nate's kisses. His heart was pounding, for fuck's sake. Was he really angry with Nate because this was what he'd wanted the whole time?

This is not okay. This is against the rules. If anyone found out...

But he let that thought die. Nate's mouth had gone softer, inviting him in, and he kept making this noise, almost a whine, like wasn't getting enough. Enough of the kiss? Enough of Dash? Dash pushed his jaw forward to give him more.

Nate's arms tightened around Dash's neck, and Dash slid an arm around his slim, firm waist.

They couldn't be doing this. If anyone found out, he could lose his job. He shuddered bodily.

I could lose my role as Prince Justice.

Just the thought was enough to break the spell. Dash pulled back.

"No," Nate murmured, trying to pull Dash in for a third time. Dash resisted, although his body very much wanted to give in. He pulled away from Nate's arms. It was almost painful to leave Nate, to break his grip.

"We can't," Dash said, like a broken stage whisper. "*I* can't."

Nate nodded and licked his lips. They looked redder, maybe a little swollen. Suddenly, Dash wanted to sink his teeth into the thickest part of his lower lip. He wanted so much.

"B-because it's against the rules?" Nate asked. He made it sound like they were in school and they were talking about something as innocuous as passing notes.

"Yes." Dash pushed himself away from the wall and stalked to the other side of the room. He rubbed his mouth as if he could erase the kiss. As if he couldn't still taste the trace of cherry soda on Nate's breath.

"No one has to know," Nate said. Dash shook his head at that, but he couldn't quite bring himself to look at him. He wasn't quite ready to see Nate's eyes again.

"This can't happen. That was just–" he broke off, trying to think of the right word. Wonderful? Fulfilling? Dreamy? No. "A mistake."

Nate moved behind him, coming closer.

"I... I mean, It didn't feel like a mistake to me. It felt pretty good."

"It *was* a mistake," Dash said, with as much force and finality as he could muster. He turned, trying to stop Nate coming closer with a glare.

Nate stopped in his tracks. "Okay. It was a mistake." He raised his hands, palms toward Dash in surrender.

God, the things he wanted to do to him. Run his hands through his hair, grab those wrists and pin him back against the wall, press his body against his until they were both breathless.

No, I have to stop thinking like this.

"Right. And you have training to complete, if we're ever going to whip you into the proper prince shape."

Nate smiled lopsidedly and opened his mouth.

Why was he smiling? Oh crap -

"And no jokes about whipping!" Dash barked.

Nate's eyes fell and his smile vanished.

"Right. Training." He looked away from Dash and rubbed at the short hairs at the base of his skull.

"Walk like actual royalty, if you can manage it." He fixed his own posture and swiped his arm across his mouth again. "Which I doubt."

Dash was laying it on thick and he wasn't sure if it was for Nate's benefit or his own. He picked up his water bottle. He briefly considered pouring the water over his head to really snap him out of the desire to kiss Nate, but that would probably be overkill.

He took a sip from the bottle and turned back to Nate, who was staring at him, his eyes wide and his expression confused. Dash's mouth went dry and he drained the bottle, before clearing his throat.

"Walk! Now!"

11 /NATE

DASHIEL MADE NATE WALK UNTIL HIS FEET WERE SORE AND HIS LOWER back ached from holding himself perfectly upright. He had, at least, got the knack of it by the end, although he privately thought he'd give Valor a bit more swagger. Dude fought dragons after all.

Then Dashiel handed him a foam sword and taught him the basics of Fairyland-approved stage fighting. This was even more exhausting because Dashiel was relentless, drilling him over and over on the basic moves.

"Are you sure I need to know all those different moves?" Nate asked, panting. Dashiel used Nate's distraction to disarm him with a flick of his wrist.

Nate sighed and went to pick up his sword for the hundredth time.

"Yes. You may have to do a sword fight in a stage show, or as part of the parade. If you do the same two thrusts and parries over and over, the audience will notice."

"Will they?" Nate scrunched up his nose. He was pretty sure people came to the park to immerse themselves in make-believe and to ride roller coasters, not to pick holes in the performance of the characters. Dashiel rolled his eyes.

"We have people who come here every day. We have

Instagrammers making money by selling guides to this place, and we have devoted fans filming everything we do. Parade videos, meet and greets, walking from A to B. They have Reddits and blogs and that's not even scratching the surface of how deep people go." Dashiel said, as if it were obvious.

"Okay?" Nate frowned. He couldn't see where Dashiel was going with this, but he seemed very intense about it. It was the most passionate he'd seen him be since the kiss incident. Nate felt a little flutter of excitement.

"Do you want to be remembered as a great Prince Valor or do you want to become a meme where someone films something you've messed up and puts silly music over it as it loops?"

Nate shivered - the kind of shiver his grandmother would have said 'someone just walked over your grave' about. "The first one."

"Right, so you do everything you can to prevent that meme from happening. You be the best you can be, and you learn everything you can."

Nate nodded. Dashiel's spiel lined up pretty well with what he'd been hoping to do anyway. He took a deep breath and brought his sword up in the guard position.

"Show me again."

Once Dashiel was satisfied that Nate knew what he was doing with the sword, it was time for dancing.

For this, Dashiel brought in Ariana and Greer.

"Hey, you two! You killed each other yet?" Greer trilled as they came in.

"How're you doing?" Ariana asked. She walked over to Nate and gave him a kiss on the cheek. "You look exhausted."

"He's been working hard," Dashiel said, giving Greer a quick one-armed hug. She screwed up her nose and pushed him away.

"Ew, sweaty!" she cried, and Dashiel chuckled.

Nate was happy to see them, of course he was. He liked Greer and Ariana, he didn't want to resent them coming into the room.

He was relieved they'd broken the tension between him and Dashiel. But breaking the tension felt like something ending. Like, even though Dashiel'd said it wouldn't happen again, maybe it was going to. Maybe he was going to be weak and kiss him again and things would've been amazing, but now the girls were here and there was no chance of it.

Now that they weren't alone in the room together the moment between them was closed off, as sure as slamming the door, and if Dashiel was to be believed, there'd never be another moment.

12 / DASH

DASH AND GREER MET UP IN THE AIRLOCK AT THE END OF THE DAY. After the dance lesson, Dash had run Nate through some basic greetings and what language he could and could not use. He was surprised to see Greer still at the airlock, as he had thought the Princesses had gone out into the park without him.

"You got plans tonight?" Dash asked. Greer looked over as the door to the Princess's changing room flung open. Ariana came out in her civvies, talking to someone on her headphones. She gave them both a wave and walked out into the park. Greer waved back and then turned to face Dash.

"Nope. Just another meal for one and Netflix."

Dash pulled a face, he hated the thought of her eating those processed frozen meals. "Come on home with me, I'll make you some real food."

"Can we watch a horror movie?" Greer asked. She smiled, showing all her teeth while she bounced, clasping her hands in front of him. "Please?"

Dash sighed. "Fine."

"Then you're on, my prince." Greer took his arm, even though he was now in a green polo shirt and jeans and she wore a Treasure the Unicorn and Princess Patience T-shirt she'd purchased in the park over leggings. He chuckled and led her out into the park proper, where they immediately dropped arms, not wanting to be recognized.

Dash's Prius was parked in the staff lot, and Greer made a beeline for it.

"What's on the menu this week?" Greer asked. He chuckled, waiting for her to fasten her seat belt before pulling out of the car park.

"Um, fish?" he tried to remember what was in his fridge.

Greer made a noise. He looked over and she was scrunching up her nose. "We had that last week."

"Fine, how do you feel about chicken?"

"Chicken sounds good. As long as it's free range."

"It is."

After that they had a quiet drive, both unwinding from the day.

As always, Dash let her into his modestly sized apartment. It didn't have a great amount of space, but it had a killer view looking over the Pacific Ocean. She followed him into the kitchen.

"Nate seemed to be picking up the prince stuff quickly," Greer said. "How'd your training session go?"

Dash's breath caught, vividly he remembered the feel of Nate's body against his, pinned between him and the wall. The cherry soda taste of his mouth.

Greer was discreet, she would never rat them out to management, he knew that. But he wasn't even sure how to describe what had happened between them.

He bent to pick up a restaurant menu that had fallen off the fridge. He put it back on the fridge, carefully lining it up square with the menu next to it and made sure the magnet was holding it before moving away.

"Sessions are going fine," he lied. Even to him the words rang hollow.

"There was kind of a weird vibe when Ari and I came in," she said. "You boys getting along okay?"

"Yeah, getting along fine." His second lie. She was bound to notice something was up.

"Uh huh, very convincing." Greer moved closer to him and touched his shoulder, encouraging him to relax. "So what happened?"

"He's just so annoying," Dash said. He sighed as he leaned against the kitchen counter.

Greer tilted her head to one side and gazed at him softly.

"Care to elaborate? What'd he do that's so annoying? Is he going off book and making Valor a rap artist?" She hauled herself up onto the kitchen counter and dangled her feet.

He tried not to shudder, and instead tugged on her arm. "Get down from there, it's not sanitary."

"Grouch." She slid down off the counter, rolling her eyes.

"He's listening fine," Dash paused again. His chest tightened and he knew he had to let out his confusion to her.

How much should I tell her? She's going to keep on asking and prodding until I spill. I should just tell her. Maybe she can help me make sense of it.

"He's... he's doing really well actually, we just had..." Dash sighed. He couldn't keep this from her, he knew she'd find out sooner or later. "We had a moment."

Greer's eyes widened, her nostrils flared and she smiled in a gentle 'Fairyland Princess' way. He could see she was controlling her reaction for his benefit.

"A moment? That sounds like it calls for wine." Greer went to the fridge and pulled out one of the bottles of Dash's favorite Riesling that he kept for special occasions. Then she went to the cabinet for wine glasses.

Dash started to prepare dinner, chopping onions and garlic and tossing them into a large pan on the stovetop. Greer put a glass down beside him – one that was far fuller than it should've been.

"Spill."

"It was when we were doing the walk," he said, mostly to the pan.

"Of course, the walk is everything." Greer wasn't often sarcastic so Dash could usually pick it up. Was she being sarcastic about the walk? He didn't think so.

He plowed on. "So, I was correcting him, and he wasn't getting it, and we had a fight."

"Like, a *fight* fight? With fists and things?" Greer raised her eyebrows, clearly surprised at the thought of it, but still willing to believe he would go there. Dash felt a little hurt. Shouldn't his best friend know he was better than that?

"No, like... yelling. We didn't punch each other, we're not street punks."

Greer snorted. "What the Hell is a street punk?" Greer pressed his glass of wine into his hand, giggling. He flushed, then took a sip.

"The point is, I shoved him against the wall and then I sort of... kissed him," Dash said, a little louder than needed.

Greer stopped moving. She stared at him with wide eyes. Then she drained her wine glass and poured herself another.

"This is *so* not like you."

Dash ran a hand through his hair. "Yeah. I know. I don't know what came over me." He looked into his glass of wine and took a deep drink. Maybe the wine would make things clearer.

"When was the last time you were with someone, Dash? I know it wasn't recent."

"I – No – That's not the point. The point is that it was a mistake, and it won't happen again." He set his wine down and turned back to the onions, which had browned and stuck to the bottom of the pan. He hadn't been paying enough attention and now they were more caramelized than tender. He sighed at himself, took the pan off the heat and put a pot of water on to boil.

"Don't avoid the question, Dash. When was the last time?" Greer prodded him a little with her pinky.

Dash's gut twisted and he moved out of prodding range. "It doesn't matter, nothing can happen there. And I don't think I even like him. Besides, you know the rules." He shook his head and added salt to the water.

"How long?"

Damn it, she really wasn't going to give it up. He would have to admit it, just to get her off his back.

"Eight months," he mumbled, mostly to shut her up. He went to the fridge and pulled out two free range chicken breasts he'd bought over the weekend and a couple of heads of bok choy. He set the meat aside and rinsed the leaves in the sink. "Maybe nine."

"Well, no wonder. You must be lonely. Not to mention," she cleared her throat. "Err… *Unfulfilled*, to put it nicely."

"It's been a dry spell," he said. He put the bok choy into the hot water and stirred it with a wooden spoon. "But work's been so busy I've hardly noticed."

"Dude, you work five days a week, same as most of the rest of the world. Sure the exact days move around, but that leaves plenty of time for socializing. You could've found someone."

Dash shook his head. He put the pan back on the heat, added a chunk of butter and then laid the chicken pieces over the top.

He sighed, thinking a little before he responded. "It's not even that I kissed him. I mean, I lost control of myself, it was so unprofessional."

"Because it's been too long." Greer pulled out dinner plates and cutlery. "You should go to a club or something. Take your mind right off it. It'll probably help with that temper of yours as well."

"My temper's fine," Dash said, through gritted teeth. He consciously unclenched his jaw as he watched the chicken carefully, turning it when it browned then pulling it out of the pan as soon as it was cooked through. He plated it up with the bok choy and some fresh raw peas, and shoved a plate towards Greer.

"How long has it been for you, if you know so much?"

"Six weeks," she leaned in to inhale the steam off the plate and sighed happily. "This smells amazing, thank you."

Dash's heart sank a little at her response. How was it so easy for her and not for him? They did the same job, didn't they?

"How do you manage it so frequently?" He asked, picking up his wine glass and heading to his small dining table.

"I'm friends with all my exes," she shrugged and smiled, as if remembering something particularly pleasant.

"Okay, but how do you do that? And wait – aren't they exes for a reason?" Dash started to eat, watching her with some mystification.

"I mean, sure, but most of them are poly and willing to hook up every now and then. No strings attached." She cut a slice of chicken popped it in her mouth, humming with pleasure. "This is really good."

Although he was pleased he was able to look after her, make sure she ate some fresh vegetables at least once a week, he knew this meal wasn't his best. The onions were overcooked and he'd under-seasoned the chicken.

"It's all right." He handed her the saltshaker. His mind was flicking through the various guys he'd had one-night stands with. He didn't want to meet up with any of them again.

"Look, the fact is you're pent up. That's all you have to deal with. Then this stuff with Nate will be manageable. You'll see he's just a nice guy you can get on with, same as me and Ari."

Dash frowned, looked up at her and sighed. "Maybe?"

"I mean, he *is* super cute, though," Greer pushed a pea around her plate, looking up at him coyly. "Would it really be that bad?"

It was tempting, obviously it was tempting, and his heart thumped with hope, but he shook his head decisively. "It's off the

61

table. I could lose my job." Dash finished off his bok choy fast, without really tasting it.

"Only if the higher-ups found out." Greer bounced her eyebrows at him. "You think no one ever hooks up at Fairyland? Believe me, it happens."

Dash frowned. He'd heard a rumor or two, but he'd always dismissed them as just that.

He imagined it for a moment.

They'd work together during the day and then Dash would drive Nate home. Nate could help him cook dinner, and they could watch movies on the couch, share stories about their day. They could kiss. And go to bed together.

Except Nate would never want to do that – not after how he'd acted today. He took a sip of wine, and then another.

Nate had only been at the park for three days and he'd made friends with everyone. Him and Cody were tight, they even had some kind of special fist bump. And Cody usually had a 'no friends with the regular staff' policy – he barely said three words a day to Dash and they'd been working together years, not days.

But him? He pushed people away without meaning to. Heck, he'd never even had a relationship that had lasted more than a few months.

Dash shook his head. It would never work.

"It was a freak accident," he said. Greer was watching his face. She opened her mouth to argue, and then shook her head, smiling.

"You're not convincing me," she said. "And you spend your days acting, so you should be able to. Something else is going on here, and you're going to have to confront it eventually."

Dash shifted uneasily under her gaze.

13 /NATE

THE WARDROBE BUILDING WAS NATE'S NEW MOST VISITED PLACE IN the park. He'd had at least five fittings for the Valor costume, and he'd only been working at the park four days. He needed three identical costumes so they could be cleaned day to day and there was a backup clean one in case something happened to the one he was wearing. Teddy was also fitting him for a fourth 'safety' costume, just in case. Nate wondered exactly what they thought would happen in a day that he'd need two backups.

The two Fairyland Wardrobe tailors assigned to his character were Teddy and Molly, and Nate had become friends with them quickly.

Teddy was a bear of a man; a gentle giant with a full beard, which made Nate wonder if Teddy was really his name or if it was an incredibly appropriate nickname. He had mid-brown hair with twinkling hazel eyes. He was always cracking a joke or telling Nate stories about people who used to play Valor, or other characters they'd had to deal with. Nate liked him instantly.

Molly, on the other hand, was a thin, pale, Goth type with a severe dyed black bob and flawless winged eyeliner. She was much quieter than Teddy, but once she saw that Nate would do what he was told during fittings ('arms up', 'turn halfway', 'look up', 'swing your arm like you're wielding a sword'), she started to warm up to him. And every now and then she'd drop a cutting one-liner about life at Fairyland. She reminded him of a girl he went to high school with.

"You're weirdly quiet today, Nate," Teddy said.

"He had prince training with Dash yesterday," Molly was on her hands and knees, pinning the hem of his pants leg. Teddy pulled a face.

"Oh, yeah. That must've been pretty bad, huh?"

Bad? No. Yes. Dreamy. Impossible.

"It was…" Nate tensed, his mind flashing back to the kisses he'd shared with Dashiel in vivid detail. And then Dashiel's dismissal of it afterward. "Intense," he finished.

He knew it wasn't enough, that he hadn't said enough. Teddy was expecting him to dish, but he wasn't about to do that. Molly and Teddy exchanged a concerned glance.

"You didn't let him beat you with a stick, did you?" Teddy asked.

"What? No! Of course not," Nate said, so surprised he laughed.

"Only, I heard that's what he passed off as 'prince training' with the last Valor."

Molly tried and failed to stifle a laugh.

Nate rolled his eyes and let out an uncertain chuckle. "I don't believe that," Nate said. "You're making it up."

"It's true. When he came in for his costume fitting he had bruises right up one side. Black and blue, he was," Teddy said, although he gave Nate a wink and a reassuring smile.

"Uh huh." Nate was pretty sure Teddy was lying – or at least stretching the truth – but it was kind of comforting to think of Dashiel as a villain. It made how he'd been treated less personal.

"Yes," Molly said, in a dry tone. "Then he put itching powder in his pants and stuck the Valor sword in a bathtub of jell-o." The irony she laid into the words made it clear that this had never happened, but Nate couldn't help but giggle.

"Well, that does sound like the kind of thing he'd do," Nate said.

The door swung open and Lennon walked into the room. "I'm glad to see you're all getting on," they said.

They looked Nate up and down critically, one finger tapping their chin as they seemed to assess him. They nodded once.

"That's looking good. Will it be ready for tomorrow?" Lennon asked, finally.

"Tomorrow?" Nate said. "Why would you need it for tomorrow?"

Molly looked to Lennon. "Maybe, it'll be a rush job, though. And we would need more fitting time later on," Molly said. She sat up and eyed the costume with a frown. Then she tugged at the tunic so it sat a little better on Nate's hip and pinned it there.

"Isn't he going to do a turn in a fursuit?" Teddy asked.

"Fur?" Nate raised his eyebrows. "Nobody mentioned a fursuit to me."

"Not this time," Lennon said, shaking their head. "You see, Nate," Lennon said, finally turning to address him, "I have some great news. The magic engineers in their labs have blueprints for an animatronic dragon float. It's badass, it's really tall, and its head sways back and forth. The legs move on pistons, it roars and everything."

"And what's that got to do with me and a fursuit?" Nate asked. He could feel excitement bubbling up inside him but he didn't want to assume anything.

"Well, in the Princess Pateince movie when the dragon kidnaps her, and Valor fights it..." Lennon raised their eyebrows at Nate, letting their words trail off.

"Oh my god," Nate breathed.

"Yes!" Lennon bounced on the balls of their feet. "So, you're going straight into Prince Valor *tomorrow* and if you impress the managers in the next week or so, they're going to build that float and you and Ari will be highlighted in the parade!"

Nate's knees threatened to give out. He drew a quick breath and put his hand on his chest.

"No pressure though," Molly said. She patted Nate's foot like she might a puppy and turned to Lennon. "Seriously, what's with the huge rush?"

"They want it ready in time for Christmas," Lennon said. "These things take time to build."

"That's awesome news, bro!" Teddy said. He slapped Nate heartily on the back and Nate had to take a step to stay upright.

"Stay still," Molly chastised. Nate resettled in the new spot and tried not to move again, although his body was screaming at him to bounce around like a bunny in Springtime.

"The parade's the big time. Someone up there must really love you," Teddy said.

"*So* much more impressive than walking between other people's floats," Lennon said. "And besides that, it's a great opportunity for you. People will be watching, this is your chance to really impress everyone."

Molly cleared her throat. "Just don't screw it up," She added. "And stop moving or I'm going to pin your leg, and none of us want that."

Nate realized he'd been practically buzzing, shifting from foot to foot in his excitement. He tried to be still, focusing on how much he didn't want to be stabbed with a pin. Of course, as soon as he tried to concentrate on being still, every muscle in his body strained against him. Then horror at what Lennon had said grew inside him.

"Wait – I only get one week? What happens if I don't impress the right people?"

"I'm not sure," Lennon said. "Maybe someone else gets a new float? I'm sure they have other ideas."

Nate nodded and breathed out, his heart was racing. "What if I'm not ready?"

"Then you better get ready, fast," Lennon said. They took another look at Nate and moved closer to squeeze his shoulder. "You have autograph training after this, and if you're really worried, we can put you out for an hour as Treasure the Unicorn."

"Wait, why? How does Treasure help?"

"You get practise at meeting people, no pressure of talking to them. It's good experience for handling crowds and playing a character," Lennon said. "It takes the pressure off your debut as Valor, because you will have already been out there."

Nate bit his lower lip, uncertain.

"All the character actors do a fursuit first," Teddy said. "You will make an amazing Treasure," Teddy said.

"Plus it's not a speaking role, so way less stress, and you can go out with Ari as practice," Lennon said.

Nate's heart pounded. Maybe it was too much to be Treasure? What if he screwed up and ruined his career as Valor, before it had even begun? But he couldn't say no, now, could he?

At least he could practice meeting people, practice at being out in the park. And it was a chance to be in character. And he did love Treasure the Unicorn.

"Okay, yeah. I'll do it. Just for an hour?" Nate said, looking at Lennon.

Teddy clapped his hands, turned and ran, disappearing into a different part of the Wardrobe room.

"Just for an hour. And you don't have to walk fancy or do anything but mime," Lennon said. "And hug. People love to hug Treasure."

"You are going to be the cutest unicorn in all the land!" Teddy said, reappearing with a giant furry white Treasure the Unicorn head – golden spiral horn, fluffy rainbow mane and everything.

Nate looked at it and then did a little happy Treasure the

Unicorn dance, half to make them all laugh and half to psych himself up.

Then he felt a sting in his leg. The pins. Molly. It had happened, she'd stabbed him in the leg and it'd all been his own stupid fault.

"Ow." He winced as she pulled the pin back out of him.

"I told you not to move!" Molly said, shaking her head.

14 /DASH

"READY FOR YOUR NEXT OUTING? YOU'LL HAVE A SPECIAL GUEST along," Lennon asked. Dash looked up. He was alone in the changing room aside from Eric and Tristan who were recovering from a stint out in the park as Autumn the Deer and Summer the Squirrel. All three looked over at Lennon, who ushered in someone dressed in the Treasure the Unicorn costume.

"Um, Okay?" Dash said. "I'm five minutes off being ready, but I can hurry."

He'd been enjoying the non-Nate time today. Nate had been in Wardrobe and other Valor-specific training that didn't require Dash. It was like he had room to breathe again.

"Who's in the suit?" Eric asked. The person in the Treasure costume planted their shiny hoof gloves on either side of their head and went to lift it off.

"No!" Lennon quickly pushed their hands away. "You can't take your own head off, remember? It's the way it's fitted on."

Treasure's shoulder slumped. A muffled 'sorry' came from inside the suit.

"It's Nate," Lennon said. They got the head off him and Nate, looking excited and a slightly flushed grinned at the room. "He's having a crash course in meet and greet etiquette so he can go out as Valor tomorrow."

Dash's chest tightened and he felt his shoulders tense. He puffed his breath out and tried to relax, he didn't want people noticing his reaction.

"Oh, that's awesome!" Eric said, jumping up. Tristan and he hurried over to Nate and starting giving him tips about how to be the character and wear the suit. Lennon stayed there too, to make sure they weren't misleading him.

Suppressing an annoyed shudder, Dash sat back in his chair, waiting for a moment, then he turned to the mirror to ensure he looked okay for a meet and greet. He adjusted a hair that had gone out of place.

Why did Nate get all the luck?

When Dash'd been cast he'd had to have one full week of training before he was allowed anywhere near a costume. Then it was at least a month as Sparkles the Friendly Dragon before he was approved for prince training.

But no, Nate didn't have to handle the unwieldy dragon wings or the long tail with the mind of its own. That damn tail which was always in danger of knocking kids over. He was shorter and cuter and everyone liked him, so he got to be the unicorn.

Mind you, it had been months since the park had a Valor, and they were sure to be missing him. Guests asked Ari about him all the time and she had to say things like 'he's visiting another kingdom' or 'he went fishing'.

Still, it was still unusual for anyone to be fast-tracked so much. Sure, Lennon and Neve had been watching Nate's work as a handler and he'd been doing an okay job – a great job, really. But that was totally different to being a character.

Dash picked up an eyeliner pencil for a touch-up and leaned forward on one elbow.

His stomach tensed, roiling, knotting. He frowned at himself in the mirror.

It was a blessing I didn't do more than kiss Nate before I shut things down. I can stand Nate being on this rocket fuel accelerated programme if he's my rival...But if he'd been my boyfriend? No. It wouldn't bare thinking about.

Dash gasped, surprised by a sudden crunching noise. He blinked furiously. Without meaning to, he had snapped his eyeliner pencil.

He set it down and took a few deep breaths.

He couldn't go out as Justice angry. That was one of his cardinal rules. Whatever was going on in Dash's head, he left it here in the changing room. Once he went out the door of the airlock, he was Justice. He was calm, friendly, kind. He was sweet, noble and charming.

His heart continued to pound. The breathing wasn't working to calm him down. His annoyance was getting tangled up with the memory of their kiss, and his sense of unfairness over everything was overwhelming him.

He opened the top drawer under the bench of his station and looked at the cards and letters from fans he'd saved over the years. He kept them on hand for just such a situation. He dug through them until he found one he hadn't looked at for a while. It was a handmade card with a wobbly approximation of Prince Justice and Princess Honesty drawn on the front, carefully colored in with felt tip markers. Inside the message read:

I love you, Prince Justice. Thank you for coming to my birthday.

It was signed 'Kelly' and Dash smiled, reading it over a few times and then tracing his finger over the words. Kelly had been one of his make a wish kids. She'd been in late stages of Leukemia, and the foundation had paid for her to tour the park, ride whatever rides were gentle enough for her, and arranged for a special Princes and Princesses party. It had been her birthday, her last one, and one of the greatest days Dash had spent as Prince Justice.

His breathing slowed down and his heart felt good again. At

peace. This was why he did it. Not for park politics. Not to be fast tracked at being promoted. For the kids.

Dash checked himself in the mirror once more and stood up.

"Come on then, Treasure, let's find the princesses and meet some kids," he said, heading towards the door.

Eric and Tristan moved back.

"You'll be great!" Tristan said.

"Remember not to speak!" Eric added.

Nate-as-Treasure gave them the thumbs up, which was mostly just a 'hoof up' and nodded at Dash, gesturing for him to lead the way. Dash felt a little uncomfortable accepting this kind gesture for him, but it'd be much more uncomfortable to turn it down.

Greer and Ariana were waiting in the airlock, ready to go in full princess mode. They both smiled wide, seeing the two of them walk out together.

"Aw, doesn't he look so cute?" Greer clasped her hands to her cheeks. She probably would have bounced but the dress weighed her down.

"Is it really Nate in there?" Ariana asked.

"Really truly," Lennon said. "Now let's make this a quick hour, or maybe just forty-five minutes. We'll see how we go."

Treasure put a hoof on Lennon's shoulder, squeezed it, and cocked their head to one side. Treasure was genderless, so even though Dash knew that Nate was inside – or whoever was playing Treasure on any given day – once they were in character, Dash automatically thought of them as 'they'.

Lennon looked at Treasure's face and their shoulders relaxed. The corners of their mouth twitched into a smile. Dash's stomach twisted again.

Damn, he's even charming when you can't see his face?

"It's okay, I'm not going to stop you. Go on, go charm some kids," Lennon said, chivvying Treasure towards the door. Nate hurried with a bit of a skip thrown in, making the princesses giggle.

"Let's head to the Rose Garden out the front of the castle, there should be enough room for this big a group," Neve said. She'd been listening to her earpiece and making hushed conversation with someone. "Sounds like it's busy out that way, so we should get a bit of an audience."

"Roger that," Lennon waited for Nate to negotiate the door in the unicorn head and then nipped around him to take the lead to the gate.

"Simon's busy right now, but he should be over as soon as he's done with his current group," Neve added.

Cody appeared by Dash's side. "Maybe I should come too. The park might be busy and you're such a big group."

"Sure, up to you," Lennon said. "I'm sure it's not going to be dangerously busy on a Thursday afternoon."

Cody's eyes twinkled with amusement and he gave Dash one of his rare grins. "I just want to watch my boy Nate here prance around some."

Dash's stomach knotted up again.

Why was Cody calling Nate his boy? Why was he making an exception and leaving his usual post in the airlock? Did everyone really like Nate that much?

Greer's arm rested on his and he forced himself to refocus.
Noble. Calm. Kind. Noble. Calm. Kind.

He steeled himself, lifting from the core and putting his shoulders back. *This was going to be a long hour.*

15 /NATE

THE PARK WAS BUSY AND THE AFTERNOON SUN BEAT DOWN, reflecting back off the concrete pathways. The heat outside the airlock took his breath away.

It was full body fur, from shoes to the head. And the head was heavy, already pushing into his shoulders. He was sweating heavily even before they left the air-conditioned airlock. Teddy had warned him this would happen, so under the suit he was wearing fitted workout leggings and a T-shirt. He hoped the fabric was all that special moisture-wicking stuff – the suit hadn't smelled when he'd pulled it on, so either the undergarments Teddy had given him were magical, or they had brilliant cleaning methods for the suits.

Nate's mind whirled through the deluge of advice he'd just been given about being Treasure from Lennon and Eric and Tristan:

Minimize your size as much as possible, so kids don't get freaked out.
No talking – EVER
Don't be too mischievous, just a little.
Be a kind unicorn.
Don't hug for too long.
No autographs, since he hadn't done the autograph training.

Become Treasure.

Don't be surprised if someone punches you, just try and get away and let security handle it.

And he added an item of his own: *Don't think about how gorgeous Dashiel looks in his suit.* That, or the possibility that Cody was just flirting with him. And how was he supposed to feel about Cody waiting until he was dressed like a unicorn before he'd made a move?

Don't think of anything but the encounter.

Oh yeah, and don't pass out.

His heart pounded, and his mind raced. Nate was reminded of the unpleasant month when he'd tried hot yoga. Wearing a unicorn suit was like walking around in a private, body-sized hot yoga studio. Only he couldn't stop for a drink of water or to wipe his face.

Nate realized just how limited his sight was in the Treasure costume as they navigated their way through the crowds to the Rose Garden. He could see directly in front of him, but his peripheral vision was severely impeded. He had so many blind spots, so the whole time he concentrated on following Lennon and hoping they wouldn't stop suddenly. He tried to skip a little at least so no one would notice that Treasure wasn't waving back to them.

Neve arranged them in a line with a few feet in between so people could come and meet them individually. Greer was in the middle, with Ariana next to her and Prince Justice on her other side. Nate was guided to a spot next to Ariana.

As with every other time Nate had come out for a character meet and greet, they had attracted a crowd of interested guests on the walk over. Even more people queued up as they got themselves into position. Being the center of attention was a different experience to being a handler. Nate lifted his chin, and the heavy unicorn head, looked at the queue and waved a hoof. A few kids waved back.

In front of him he could see Cody, who'd moved to the side of the queue, staying back a little but keeping the line orderly every now and then with a gesture or a comment.

Nate took a deep breath as the first group approached them. It was a woman with a little baby. The woman beamed at him and his heart melted. He knew how to handle this, babies were adorable. And a baby with a unicorn? He might have to track down a photo himself.

"Hi, Treasure! This is Dylan, smile Dylan!" Nate waved at the baby and then looked toward the man holding up the phone and snapping pictures of the woman and Dylan. He cocked his head a little so Treasure would look cute in the photos.

The woman shoved the baby towards his head and kind of mashed the baby's face against his furry nose. He reached up a hoof-gloved hand and patted the baby gently.

"Thanks, Treasure," the woman said. She moved to the side to presumably do the same thing with Ariana.

Something in the middle of Nate's back released and his shoulders relaxed. He hadn't realised how tense he was, but he'd survived his first encounter just fine.

The next group came up, and then the next, and time blurred as Nate got into the swing of it, waving and posing and giving hugs. This was easy, he could do this. Everyone he interacted with left with a smile, and he was feeling invincible, on top of the world. King of the park.

Until it all came crashing down with one guest.

"Got any boobs under there?" The guy hugging him hissed, groping his chest through the fur.

Nate instinctively took a step back, colliding with a perfectly manicured rosebush. He stumbled and would've fallen except the guy who'd just grabbed him caught his elbow and righted him with a smirk. Nate pulled his arm away as soon as he was steady on his feet again, shuddering and hoping it wasn't obvious through the suit.

Nate's insides screamed. What was this guy playing at? Who would come to Fairyland and do... *that*? Everything inside him urged him to shove the guy, or punch him, or give him a lecture on how to treat people, regardless of whether or not they had breasts. But he was trapped as Treasure. He couldn't speak, he couldn't do anything to upset the guests, and he most definitely couldn't do something that would look bad on camera. Nate swallowed and waved at the next person in line, beckoning them forward.

Just as the creeper guy moved away, he turned to keep half an eye on what he did with Ariana. But apparently, the guy was just a creeper about unicorns – he seemed to be well behaved with the others.

Nate's hands shook. Lennon had warned him that something could happen, but he didn't expect it right off the bat, on his first outing as a Fairyland character.

Was this what he could expect from every shift going forward?

It was so hot and sweaty in the costume he was having trouble thinking straight.

"Everyone get together, group photo with the Richmonds!" Someone said. Nate couldn't see who it was, and then Lennon approached from his blind spot, startling him some.

"Come on Treasure, this way," Lennon said. "Come pose with the prince and princesses." Lennon guided him into place, and he went down to one knee to pose with the kids in the family.

The kids were very sweet. One little boy looking up at him with an excited smile.

"Treasure, excuse me, but is it okay if I stroke your mane?"

Nate nodded and leaned his head down so the little boy could reach it.

"It's so soft!" He giggled. The other kids crowded in to pet Nate's unicorn head as well.

"This way please, smile for the camera!" Someone shouted, cheerily. Nate heard the voice as if it was calling from the other end of the park. He frowned, shaking his head slightly to clear his brain fog. He knew that voice. It was someone he'd heard before..

Simon! Simon the photographer.

The kids moved back into position and Nate righted himself. He got a head rush and sucked in a breath. That wasn't good.

When had his ears started ringing? It was so hot.

The family moved off and Nate tried to get to his feet again, but it wasn't as easy as it should've been. He could feel himself swaying, and the voices nearby were hard to hear. There was a buzzing noise over them. He swung his head around, trying to find Lennon to signal there was something wrong.

"I think I need to take Treasure to the Enchanted Forest."

He knew that voice too, but it wasn't the same voice from before.

It was Dash. Dash who didn't want to kiss him. Dash who said he couldn't call him Dash.

"Come on, Treasure!" He sounded so cheerful. Nate felt a strong hand tug on his hoof, and then he was walking in the same direction he was being tugged. That was fine. He couldn't exactly lift his feet off the ground, but he could move where he was being guided.

Nate concentrated on putting one foot in front of the other. He saw some other feet nearby, and he lifted his head with some effort to see whose feet they were. Cody's. Cody was there. Nate sighed. Cody was nice. Scary, but nice. He could probably tear an arm of someone if he really wanted to, but Cody was his friend, so he wouldn't do that to Nate.

Nate tried to figure out where they were going, but they were in a part of the park he didn't recognize. Dash was still holding onto him. Wait, did Dash change his mind? Did Dash want to kiss him again?

A kiss would be nice.

"We clear?" Dash's voice sounded urgent. Nate wondered

what was so important. Perhaps Dash had a single hair out of place? That would be a *disaster*.

"Not clear," Nate mumbled. He imagined Eric and Lennon's voices in his head.

*Don't speak! No matter wha*t! He hoped nobody had heard him say that.

"Yup, out of visibility."

"Can you get him some water or something, please?"

Someone's feet ran away. Was it Cody's feet? Or Dash's? *Bam, bam, bam* they were running fast.

Someone's hands were fiddling with something on Nate's costume. From when he'd put it on, Nate remembered that there were straps and bits of Velcro. Then the Treasure head was being lifted off him. Panic. He scrambled to grab at the head and shove it back down. He couldn't be seen with the head off!

"No, I'm supposed to–" Nate tried to get the words out. Then he was thrust into the bright sunlight, breathing fresh air. "Christ, that's good."

Dash's face swam into focus, standing over him. His eyebrows were drawn together, almost like he was worried. He placed a hand on Nate's forehead and nodded.

"Heat exhaustion, I knew it. Just try and breathe. How do you feel?"

"I think the bees buzzing in my head are gone," Nate said, but he wasn't sure if he was speaking as clearly as he should be. "But now my head hurts. Like. Really hurts." He touched his own forehead and groaned softly.

Cody came back with a bottle of bright blue sports drink.

"Drink this, Nate," Cody said. He shoved the bottle towards him but realized he couldn't take it – he still had a hoof instead of a hand. Cody popped the drink open and fed a little to Nate, who swallowed gratefully. The cold blue drink flooded his system. He didn't usually like sports drinks but this one was absolutely delicious, and he'd never been thirstier. It was the best drink in the world.

Dash unzipped the back of the suit and pushed it off Nate's shoulders.

"You tryin' to get me naked?" Nate giggled, but he could tell his voice was wavering.

Cody laughed and as soon as Nate had a hand free of the glove, Cody gave him the bottle.

"You can head back, Dash. I'll get him back safely," Cody said.

"No, you go and let Lennon know he's okay. They have the princesses there, they'll be fine," Dash said. He sounded authoritative.

"I already updated Lennon over the earpiece," Cody said. "But... if you're sure?"

"I'm sure," Dash said. "I'll get him back."

Were they fighting over him? Had Dash just won the fight? Why had they fought? Why had Dash wanted to win?

Nate pressed the condensation-soaked bottle against his forehead. It felt like putting his head into a fridge at the end of a run. He took another drink. He could feel his head clearing up, slowly.

"Thanks for fighting for me," he said to Dash.

Dash raised his eyebrows. "What?"

"Kissing's really good, and kissing you was amazing," Nate said. He swallowed. Had he said that out loud? Dash's eye twitched.

Yeah, I said that out loud. Nate dropped his eyes and tried to sink into the ground.

16 /DASH

"Don't drink it all at once," Dash said. His heart was pounding. First from fear for Nate and the heat stroke or whatever he had, and then because he mentioned kissing. He wanted to divert the conversation to a safe place. "Just take little sips, slowly."

"Right," Nate said. He took a small sip of the drink and then another.

Dash bundled the Treasure head under one arm. It had been a mistake to send Nate out unprepared on such a hot day. Even in his Justice costume he was hot, and Nate'd had no experience in fur. They should've made sure he was well hydrated and had a cooling pad or something in the head. He sighed, shaking his head. He'd have to have a word to Lennon.

Nate stepped out of the last parts of the Treasure suit. Underneath, he was wearing compression athletic pants and a T-shirt which was half sweat-soaked.

It shouldn't have looked hot but...

Dash forced his gaze down. He picked up the rest of the suit and wadded it up.

"I've got it," Nate said, reaching for the suit. Dash shook his head.

"No, it's fine. You just keep drinking, you need to recover."

"Um, okay," said Nate, taking another sip. "Thanks for this, Dash – I mean, Dashiel,"

"It's okay," Dash sighed, unsure if he meant it was okay for Nate to call him Dash, or if it was okay that he had got him out of the meet and greet.

"How'd you know I needed rescuing?"

Dash's stomach rolled uncomfortably. "Come on, let's get you to the air conditioning," Dash didn't want to think about rescuing Nate – it sounded far too romantic. He didn't even want to think about why he'd been so insistent that he should be the one to look after Nate, not Cody.

"How'd you know?" Nate asked again.

Dash shrugged, trying to play it off as no big deal. "I've worked here a long time. I could see the signs. You were swaying, you put your head down for those kids, and that can make your head swim even on a cooler day when you're in a suit like that. Come on, out of the hot sun," he led the way down the pathway through the trees and behind the castle.

"Where even *are* we?" Nate asked.

"This is an access way. It's mostly used by the cleaners or the photographers. It's a bit of a roundabout way back, but I figured you'd want out of the suit as fast as possible."

"You figured right," Nate said, his voice a bit slurred again. "You're a good figurer."

Dash couldn't help but feel a flash of protectiveness and affection. He tried to squash it down or ignore it.

"Sure. Sip your drink, Nate." He glanced back to make sure Nate was following close behind. Even although he was concerned for him, Nate was kind of cute like this. Like he was slightly drunk, or like he'd just woken up from a deep sleep. He was a little soft, a little vulnerable.

Yet Dash couldn't quiet the tiny, nasty voice in the back of his head that was happy. Because this had been one of Nate's trials, hadn't it? And he'd failed it spectacularly.

Even so, he couldn't help but feel relieved that he'd been close enough to catch Nate before he keeled right over. If Treasure had fainted in front of all those people it'd be bad press. People could've said he was drunk or on drugs in the park or something.

He looked back to catch Nate breathing heavily. "You okay to walk?"

"Yeah, I am," Nate said, looking up at him, his eyes glassy.

Dash frowned. "Let me know if you need a break or rest or something."

"I'm okay, just keep walking. I'm dying to get to that air con you promised."

There was a pause in the conversation as they walked, Dash was glad for it at first. But once they had navigated a couple of forks in the path a nagging voice in his head suggested maybe Nate needed a little reassurance.

"Listen, don't worry too much about this," he said. "We have fur characters passing out all the time. Lennon should've known it was too hot out for a first-timer."

"So stupid, I feel so stupid," Nate mumbled.

"What was that?" Dash slowed down and looked over his shoulder at him.

"I'm stupid. I failed right away. Now I'll never get to be on a dragon float," Nate had the same kind of tone as a pouting child. Dash rolled his eyes and ignored what he was saying, assuming he was just a little heat silly still.

"It's gonna be okay, this stuff happens."

"No, the... I messed up." He looked so pathetic, Dash's heart ached for him. He had to reassure him that he wasn't to blame.

"It's okay, no one's going to judge you on this," Dash said. He adjusted his hold on the Treasure costume. Lennon was to blame, if anyone was. He'd definitely be having that word with them.

Dash led Nate into the backlot and up to the back entrance to Wardrobe.

"Oh, sweet air conditioning!" Nate exclaimed. He swigged from his drink bottle and sighed happily.

Teddy looked up. "Is that Nate back already?" He called out.

"I nearly *died*," Nate said, his eyes wide. "But Dash rescued me because he's a handsome prince."

"You didn't nearly die – you got heat exhaustion," Dash handed the Treasure costume to Teddy, rolling his eyes for effect. "He'll need to lie down for at least half an hour, and he'll need to keep taking liquids."

Molly hurried over and slipped her arm around Nate, pulling his arm over her shoulders. "Come on, you can come rest on my tizzy couch."

She led him over to the chaise longue which was partially covered in pieces of cloth.

"He'll be okay," Teddy said, coming over to pat Dash's shoulder. "Don't worry about him. And he needs a final fitting anyway. Once he's feeling better, we'll finish that up."

"I'm not worried about him." Dash's voice cracked, betraying the fact that yes, he was very worried about Nate, even though he'd more or less handed him over to Molly and Teddy. He watched as she helped Nate recline on the couch, he looked so vulnerable. Surely Nate needed Dash to hang around and look after him?

Teddy still had his hand on Dash's shoulder, so he shrugged it off. "Thanks, Teddy," he said. He had to leave, and make sure there was some distance between them. Nate had brought up kissing again which meant it was still on his mind. Dash couldn't think about that. He left the room, forcing himself not to look back and check on Nate again.

17 /NATE

"You're gonna rock it!" Charlie slapped Nate's thigh as they drove into Fairyland. "First week! No one even *dreams* of making it to Prince in the same week they start at Fairyland."

"I know you think you're helping but you're kinda just freaking me out," Nate replied. He was chewing his lower lip – then remembering he had to look perfect and stopping – and then chewing it again because he was a bundle of nerves.

"You're gonna be fine. What do you need from me? You want me to tell you you're pretty?"

Nate laughed. "Yes. No. Distract me, tell me how things have been in the restaurants."

"Same as they ever were," Charlie said. He sighed and ran a hand through his hair, he looked tired. "I've been trying to push the higher ups to let me make some changes to the menu but it's so hard to convince anyone around here to try something new."

"Maybe I should go in there, everyone seems excited to give me new things," Nate said, only half joking. Charlie smiled wide.

"I mean, maybe. Come visit as Prince Valor and demand a spiced rack of lamb or a gently pan-fried bit of fish with garlic butter."

"Yeah, I'll absolutely do that on my first day as Valor when I'm being watched by the managers or whoever makes the decisions," Nate said, laughing. "But who knows? Maybe once I've been doing it a month or so?"

"Oh, I'll hold you to that," Charlie winked. He pulled the car into the car park and they said goodbye to each other.

Nate still wasn't used to being allowed into the park early. And the staff who waved at him and greeted him by name. He was still in love with the park, the weird encounter as Treasure notwithstanding.

He made his way to the secret path and let himself into the airlock.

"Morning, Nate!" Cody sat at one of the tables eating a Danish. "Teddy's been in already with something fancy in a garment bag. I think he left again, but he might just be lurking, I dunno."

"Isn't it your job to know these things?" Nate asked. He reached over to try and steal a piece of pastry but Cody slapped his hand.

"No, it's my job to keep you all safe, not to monitor everyone's every movement." He relented, tore off a piece of pastry and offered it to Nate, who took it gratefully.

Dashiel walked in. He had a huge Starbucks cup and dark sunglasses on. "Morning all." He pushed his sunglasses up on top of his head and looked between Cody and Nate, frowning slightly before heading for the changing room.

"Hey, Dash," Cody replied.

Nate moved away from the table to follow Dashiel into the changing room. "Hey, thanks for what you did yesterday. I know I was a bit out of it. I'm, um... sorry if I said anything inappropriate."

"Don't mention it," Dashiel said. He set his cup and sunglasses down on the makeup table. He didn't meet Nate's eyes. "As long as you didn't keel over onto a kid, we're good."

Nate took a couple of steps towards him. He wanted to say

more. He wanted to say that even though Dashiel could be an asshole, he could see that he was a caring guy under it. He wanted to say that he wanted Dashiel to act out some steamy scenes from one of Nate's favorite fanfics for him. He wanted to, but he bit his lip. It wasn't going to be like that, and he had to stop thinking like being with Dashiel was a possibility. Daydreams were fine, but he couldn't let them get in his way.

Being Valor was a dream come true – it was too important to him mess up with a silly crush.

"There you are, Your Majesty!" Teddy's voice was unmistakable, echoing through the changing room. He grinned at Nate, sweeping his hand across his waist and bending into a low bow. "Your royal vestments await!"

Dashiel shook his head and sat down at his station, ignoring them.

Once Nate was in costume and his hair and makeup had been done by Teddy and Molly, Lennon came in to check on him.

"How're you doing?" They asked.

"He's fine. He got to sleep last night – unlike some of us," Molly said. Groaning, she collapsed into Nate's chair and pulled her sunglasses back on.

"You're assuming a lot there," Nate said. He swallowed and gave Lennon a big smile. "I'm good."

"Yeah, really convincing," Lennon said. Lennon looked him over with a critical eye. Tugged on the sleeve of the shirt on one side, rubbed at his eyebrow with their thumb. He tried to stay still under their ministrations.

"Sorry... I'm nervous as Hell."

"Language!" Teddy did his best to look appalled. "This is *Fairyland!*"

"I'm nervous as, uh, a rabbit during hunting season?" Nate said, wondering if that would be an acceptable substitute.

Lennon squeezed his shoulder and gave him a tight smile.

"You don't need to be nervous. You've seen how this place works."

Nate picked up his new water bottle and took a swig. "Yeah, I guess." He had serious butterflies in his stomach, but he tried to sound confident.

"You'll be fine, which reminds me. Dash?" Lennon called out. Dashiel swung around in his chair, looking impatient. "You're gonna look after Nate out there, right?"

Nate studied Dashiel's face, taking another sip from his bottle as he did. He wanted to see a sign of something, some emotion… kindness? Sympathy? Affection, maybe?

"Of course," Dashiel said. His voice was light, and he looked Lennon in the eyes before throwing Nate a quick smile. It wasn't quite sincere, but it was professional. "We're a team out there."

Tension drained out of Nate's body and some of the butterflies evaporated from his stomach. Dashiel had been there for him when he'd had heat exhaustion. Nate knew that he'd be there for him today. Even if there was some weirdness between them, Dashiel would be professional.

Nate took a deep breath in. So now he just had to worry about staying hydrated and being charming.

He could do that.

"Ari will help you too, obviously. Probably after a week we can send just the two of you out together."

As Nate nodded, he couldn't help looking over at Dashiel again, but he'd already turned back to the mirror, eyebrow pencil in hand.

"Do the princes ever go out together? Like, without their pairing?" Nate knew the answer, but he asked it all the same. Because just he and Dashiel might be a lot of fun.

"Mm-hmm, at the big events," Lennon said. They eyed Nate curiously, and Nate thought they were about to ask why he wanted to know, but Teddy saved him from awkwardness.

"Oh yes, at the Halloween party! In your Halloween-style costume!" Teddy bounced some and clapped his hands together.

"Quiet!" Molly pouted, waving one hand. "I'm trying to nap."

"Lots of characters do different stuff for seasonal events," Lennon said. "Christmas greetings time, too – we like to mix it up to make it a bit more special."

"I've never been to any of those events," Nate said. "I bet they're a lot of fun." Unbidden, he imagined Dashiel in his Justice costume, lingering under the mistletoe. He shook his head to get rid of the image.

Lennon put a finger in the air, signalling they were listening to their earpiece.

Teddy took the opportunity to move in close and adjust the way Nate's costume sat on his shoulders. "You weren't symmetrical. Anything feel too tight or like it might fall off you?"

"No, it feels good, still," Nate stretched his arms up over his head, testing his movement and the fit around his biceps.

Teddy watched with a critical eye. "Hmm, your shirt rides up when you do that. I'll make the other shirts a little longer," he said.

Nate nodded, and the hairs prickled on the back of his neck. He glanced over and saw Dashiel quickly look away from him. Had he been watching him?

"We're ready. Come on, Dash! Stop primping, time to head out," Lennon called as they swept out of the changing room.

Dashiel fastened his sword belt and waited patiently as Teddy hurried to fuss over him.

"Ted, I've done this a thousand times, you really don't need to worry," he said, wearily.

"Sure you have, but Nate hasn't. I feel like a proud mama duck about to watch my ducklings jump into the water for the first time."

Nate laughed. "Is that a thing ducks do?"

"Yes, it is." Teddy frowned, plucking an invisible piece of fluff off Dashiel's shining red tunic and nodding. "You had a little Treasure fur on you," he said when Dashiel looked down.

Nate looked away. He didn't need the Treasure fiasco reminder right before he went out again.

"We'll be fine, Ted," Dashiel said. He walked over to Nate and patted his shoulder. "Besides, I trained him. He'll be perfect."

Nate's cheeks warmed again, his mind instantly flashing back to the forbidden kiss they had shared during training.

He nodded at Lennon. He stood more confidently - remembering Dashiel's training and smiled.

"Let's go."

18 /DASH

IT WAS LIKE EVERYONE IN THE PARK WAS IN LOVE WITH NATE. IT started with Teddy, then Molly, Lennon, Cody – and obviously Ari and Greer.

From the moment they left the airlock, Nate became Prince Valor. Ari was on his arm, and they walked in front of Dash and Greer. Dash used the journey to the Reflecting Lake to watch Nate's walk. It was smooth, purposeful; just like Dash had shown him. But there was a bounce to it somehow... Almost the hint of a dance.

Had he ever been trained in hip-hop? Was he a natural dancer? Whatever it was, he was doing something Dash had never seen a Fairyland prince do before.

He was making Valor cool.

It was infuriating and terrifying at the same time, but he swallowed all those swirling emotions and focused on being noble, calm and kind.

They set up for the meet and greet at the Reflecting Lake photo nook. It was a very sweet space for a photo, the cobblestones and weeping willow trees creating a natural arch. The lake behind them was carefully maintained by a team of landscapers.

Lennon and Neve arranged them in pairs, with a gap in

between. Simon set up and was guiding a new junior photographer into position – one photographer for each pairing.

Neve organized the queue so the people would meet Prince Justice and Princess Honesty first and then move across to Valor and Patience.

Of course, no one had expected there to be a Prince Valor appearance, but Dash knew that the word would already be getting out among Fairyland's most devout followers. He followed enough Fairyland social media himself to know news travelled at the speed of sound. The diehard Valor fans would be in the park as soon as they could negotiate time off work, ditch class or get in the car. For some of them, that would be within an hour.

Dash focused on the guests, but he kept an eye on Nate. Greer was watching Nate, too – he could tell. A few of the guests even asked the two of them about Prince Valor.

"Has he come back from his fishing trip, then?" A woman in her forties asked, giving Dash a knowing smile.

"Yes, we're so glad to have him back," Greer said. "Aren't we, Justice?"

"Of course, Honesty. I'm looking forward to going riding with him again," Dash smiled wide.

The guest laughed, one hand flying to her chest. "You two are so funny! Can I have a selfie?"

They posed while she took a selfie and then the woman looked over at Nate again. "He's so *handsome*," she said.

"He *is* handsome," replied Greer , nodding. Dash bit his tongue so he wouldn't agree, too. "But I think my Prince Justice is more handsome."

Dash gave the woman a smile. "I'm sure he'd love to meet you," he said. She waved goodbye to them and went across to Prince Valor and Princess Patience. Just as the next guests approached he heard the woman addressing Nate.

"Welcome back, Prince Valor! I hope you caught some big fish!"

The next twenty minutes went in much the same way, with both him and Greer fielding excitement about Valor's reappearance from the majority of the guests.

The whole time Dash felt like he had hyper-awareness, his hearing tuned into every conversation, every laugh coming from where Nate and Ari were stationed. He could sense Nate charming people. He could feel the genuineness of his interactions with the guests. Every time there was a moment between visitors, Dash would look over and watch.

At one point, Nate picked up a little boy wearing a Princess Patience dress and spun him through the air in a circle. The two of them made a charming picture, and everyone in the line was capturing it on their phones and other devices. Nate smiling wide, his eyes fixed on the little boy's face. The boy, with his hands on Nate's arms, squealed with delight.

Soon after that they were all asked to pose together with a ten-year-old girl on crutches, her right leg in a cast.

"I hope you get better soon, sweetheart," Ari said, fussing over the girl and arranging her hair for her.

"I'm Maia," the girl said. "You're really pretty, Princess Honesty."

"Well, aren't you just too lovely!" Ari practically glowed.

"I broke my leg falling off a horse!" Maia exclaimed, smiling proudly at all of them.

"Oh, dear! I've fallen off my horse before, too," Nate replied. "I broke my collarbone."

Maia winced in sympathy. Dash's heart raced. He realised he had to step up himself, he wasn't about to let Nate get all the attention.

"And you know what? Just at first, after the accident, he was afraid to go riding again," Dash went to one knee beside Maia.

Nate glanced down at him and nodded, putting a hand on Dash's shoulder. Dash could feel the warmth of his hand.

Don't think about his hand on you.

"That's right. I was afraid it would happen again, but I didn't let the fear stop me. I got right back up on Truly, and I kept on riding," Nate said.

Maia looked between them and nodded. "I don't ever want to stop riding."

"What's *your* horse's name?" Dash asked. He knew Simon would be taking pictures this whole time, so he made sure to smile and make eye contact with the girl. He'd done this a thousand times after all. He had experience on his side.

"El Diablo," the girl said. "And he doesn't let anyone but me ride him!"

"Well, I bet El Diablo is looking forward to when you ride with him again," Nate said. The girl beamed up at him.

Once the photos were taken, Dash shifted to stand up. Nate's hand squeezed his shoulder before letting go.

He's been holding onto me this whole time?

Dash didn't let anything show on his face, but he felt a flash of warmth through his chest. His heart fluttered and he glanced at Nate as he stood. So freaking handsome. No, he couldn't think about that. But he couldn't deny, that had been some Fairyland magic for sure, and they'd created it together.

19 /DASH

THE MEET AND GREET CONTINUED WELL. DASH WAS IMPRESSED WITH Nate's performance (although, of course, he noticed a couple of things he could improve on), and there had been a ripple of excitement through the park about Valor's return to the kingdom.

As soon as they were back in the airlock, Teddy grabbed Nate and took him to Wardrobe for adjustments.

Dash went to the vending machine for a cold soda. He didn't usually have soda at all, as it was best to keep his sugar intake down to avoid mood crashes or energy dips. But for once he felt a little like celebrating.

Greer was amazing, and they worked well together, but that moment with Maia and Nate had been extra. An extension. He couldn't remember the last time he'd been able to bounce off and build a story with another character in quite that way, and to make it personal to the guest as well?

It had felt next level, and he felt a buzz from it. Surely that was going to show up on someone's Instagram story, and then it'd be Fairyland history.

"Greer, Dash, can I have a word?" Lennon asked, darting into the airlock before they vanished into their respective changing rooms. He nodded, bringing his soda with him to join Greer and Lennon in the small room the handlers used as an office.

"Sure. What's this about?" Dash asked. He waited for Greer to sit and sweep her voluminous skirts out of the way before he sat down in the seat beside her.

"I just wanted to give you a heads up," Lennon said. "It's nothing bad, nothing to worry about. So don't panic."

Dash shot Greer an uneasy glance, only for it to be returned. He picked up his soda can and put it down again, then cleared his throat. He could be direct with Lennon.

"I'd prefer that when someone says it's nothing to worry about that they actually just tell me what it is," Dash said.

"Noted." Lennon replied. "Well, as you know, Nate's been shooting through our regular training practices way faster than normal,"

"What does that have to do with us?" Greer asked. Dash crossed his legs, looking at Greer. Her forehead was furrowed.

"The reason is, some of the higher-ups are watching how he does. There's a possibility of a new float in the parade, or maybe a whole new section."

"A new float?" Greer said. "I'm sorry, Lennon, I'm still not exactly following what this has to do with me and Dash."

"Well, the favored option for the new float is an animatronic dragon." Lennon pulled out a brown paper folder marked 'eyes only' and stamped with a heavy blue 'top secret' stamp. Dash had seen one or two of these folders before. They were closely guarded – new designs for the park were always treated like matters of national security.

They pulled a piece of paper out of the folder, careful to keep the rest inside, and turned it to show to Dash and Greer.

Dash leaned forward to look at float concept sketches. The float had a tower in the back, with a princess in it, waving. In the front was a huge green dragon with a long neck and wide wings. Drawn on the ground in front of the float was the figure of a prince, brandishing a sword. He was wearing blue – Valor's colors.

Dash frowned. "Dragon float," he said. Nate had said something like that when he was going loopy from the heat in the Treasure costume. Dash'd thought it'd just been nonsense, but here it was, lining up with that float for Valor and Patience rumor he'd heard. It was all falling into place.

"If Nate can impress in the next week as Prince Valor, then this float will be fast-tracked for production. It will be a featured part of the parade, and there'll probably be some dancers dressed as dragons following it, and something else in the front. I don't know. Whatever happens, it'll be impressive."

Dash's mind raced – the dragon was awesome. Nate fighting a literal dragon would look badass. His heart sank. More importantly, it would take the audience's breath away; it would stop the show. Everyone would be taking pictures and sharing them on social media. Dash clenched his jaw as he imagined just how little people would care about Princess Honesty and Prince Justice waltzing like characters on a music box after they saw a giant robot dragon.

"That's amazing," Greer said, though Dash caught a flatness to her voice. She was leaning forward. "What an incredible design. Will it really look like this?"

Lennon nodded enthusiastically at Greer. "It'll probably be better in real life."

Dash thought about every word Lennon had said. He seized on his one scrap of hope.

"If. You said *if*," he said. "What happens if Nate *doesn't* get the approval of whoever's watching?"

Lennon looked at Dash, their expression blank. "Well, if Nate doesn't excel as I expect him to, then there are other directions management will go."

Lennon gave Dash a penetrating look. Dash cleared his throat and nodded. "Right."

"But most likely this float would be made anyway, in time," Lennon said. "They want to start construction as soon as possible. The dragon would be great to have before Christmas, for example."

"It is an amazing dragon," Greer said. "I'm sorry if I'm missing the point, but I'm still not sure what this has to do with us, precisely? It seems like Nate's thing – and Ari's."

"Yes, which brings me to my point. I'll be wanting your feedback on Nate's performance, like a mini appraisal," Lennon said. They carefully filed the papers back into the folder as they spoke. "A couple of people have been assigned as mystery guests, who'll have encounters with him and report back. I haven't told Nate about that, obviously. And I'll be nearby too, but you two will be working immediately with him, so I'd like your feedback for my report."

"Oh, of course," Greer said. "That won't be a problem."

"Yes, happy to help," Dash agreed. Lennon gave him a sharp look, but he smiled back. He had an idea forming, but he couldn't let on what it was to Lennon. He had to keep it together and make them believe what he said.

Dash jumped as Lennon's landline rang. Lennon looked at the caller ID.

"I'm sorry, I have to take this."

"Of course," Dash said. He tapped his fingers on his knee and swallowed.

Keep it together.

The conversation on the phone was very short. "I'll be right there," Lennon said. As they stood up, they turned to Dash and Greer. "This will just take a moment. Please wait here and I'll give you some more details."

"No worries, take your time." Greer settled back in the chair and yawned lightly.

Lennon bustled out the door, tapping their earpiece and talking sharply. There was a moment's silence. Greer inspected her nails, but Dash couldn't tear his eyes away from the folder with 'Top Secret' stamped on it. He leaned forward. It was calling his name.

I won't do anything with the sketches, he told himself. *I just want to see what else is in there.*

He reached for the folder.

"Dash, don't…" Greer trailed off, her tone telling Dash that she was curious as well, and although she thought it was a bad idea, this was likely to be her only protest.

He pulled the folder towards him and flipped through. There were a few different sketches of the dragon float, and then a concept sketch for something quite different.

His breath caught and he tugged the sketch out.

It was from the iconic scene in *Princess Honesty and the Witch* where Justice and Honesty rode winged horses through the sky. The float had winged horses, which, from what Dash could surmise from the sketch, would flap their wings and move on mechanical arms. The base of the float resembled clouds, and there was the arch of a rainbow at the back. It wasn't as cool as a dragon fight, but still much better than the current Honesty and Justice float.

"Oooooh," Greer said. "That's pretty."

They both looked over it for a few more seconds, then Dash carefully slid it back into the folder,. He picked up his soda and sipped from it. This changed things. If Nate failed to impress, there was a chance of Dash and Greer getting a better float?

Lennon walked back in. "Sorry, just a minor mishap with Fairy Mischief's meet and greet, it's sorted now." They sat back down. "Now, about Nate. You're all right to give feedback? Both of you?"

"Yes, for sure." Greer said. Dash eyed her, trying to read her expression, but it seemed utterly calm. She was smiling at Lennon and acting as if she'd never seen any other sketches.

"He did great this morning, but we'll keep an eye out," Dash said. His heart thumped in his chest, his excitement building. He wouldn't lie about Nate's performance, but he might do something else.

"And I know you'll do whatever you can to help him." There was a certain emphasis and gravity to their words, and their eyes drilled into Dash's. Dash wondered if Lennon somehow knew he'd looked at the other float sketches, or if they could read his mind somehow. Greer looked between them and cleared her throat.

"Yes, we will. We'll ensure he does a good job."

"Great! Well that's all then, go rest up before the next meet and greet, and I'll catch up with you again before the end of next week," Lennon said.

As they left the handler's office, Dash pulled Greer aside before she vanished into the princesses changing room.

"This is a great opportunity," he said in a hushed tone. Greer looked at him with her eyebrows raised.

"Yes, it is. For *Nate*." She tugged her arm out of his grip and rubbed it, frowning.

"And for *us*. Didn't you see the Pegasus float?"

Greer looked away. "I did." She sighed. "What are you thinking? You're not going to sabotage him, are you?"

"What? No! No, of course not," Dash said. "But that doesn't mean we can't outshine him and Ari."

"Outshine how?" Greer narrowed her eyes and folded her arms.

"We can go the extra mile, you know, step it up." He bounced once on his feet, hoping she'd go for it. He took her hand and squeezed her. He could usually talk her around if he showed her how enthusiastic he was.

"I don't know, Dash. It sounds sort of… villainous." Greer chewed on her lower lip. Dash felt a glimmer of hope. The lip chewing meant she was considering it, even though she wasn't sure about the idea.

He let her think it through, giving her time to weigh up the options. Her mouth twisted to one side and then she nodded.

"Okay. We'll still help them but we'll be extra good ourselves. I can get behind that plan." She shrugged. "I mean, it'd be nice not to spin around on that float forever." She rolled her eyes but gave him an indulgent smile.

Dash gave her a quick hug, knowing better than to gloat that she'd agreed with him. "You're not going to regret it. And it's just for this week."

She nodded, and they both went to their respective changing rooms.

Dash drained the last of his soda and went to sit at his station just as Nate walked back in, tugging at the hem of his shining blue brocade jacket.

Dash stifled a secret smile. Sure, Nate was cute and all, but he had experience. And over the next week he was going to out-charm, out-noble and straight up out-prince Nate in every possible way.

20 /NATE

NATE WOKE UP ON SATURDAY MORNING FROM A DEEP, DREAMLESS sleep. His first week at Fairyland had left him more exhausted than he could ever remember being.

He'd barely stayed awake after getting home on Friday, and he'd only managed a frozen meal reheated in the microwave before passing out on the couch. He'd woken at some point in the middle of the night to grab a drink of water and drag himself to his bed – and he'd been asleep almost as soon as he'd pulled the blanket up.

He blinked. Sunlight streamed through the blinds he'd forgotten to close. His mouth was parched, and his head felt cloudy.

Something woke me up. What was it?

He sat up and rubbed the grains of sleep out of his eyes. Then he noticed a noise. A weird jingling, but a familiar weird jingling?

Oh right, phone. It was faint though, sort of muffled.

With a colossal effort he got out of bed and went out to the living area where he'd passed out. He got to it a second before it stopped ringing. Charlie. He accepted the call.

"Charlie? Yeah?"

"Hey, superstar. Guess who's arrived?" Charlie said.

"Wh-What? Are you outside? Ah, no, do we have work?" Nate's heart raced and he looked around, wondering if he had any clean underwear.

"No, it's Saturday."

"Urgh... Then why did you call so early?" Nate groaned as he fell back onto the couch.

"It's eleven, my buddy," Nate could almost hear Charlie shaking his head.

"Okay, okay. Who has arrived, what are you talking about? Are you outside my door?" Nate made a move towards his door as he spoke. He pulled the chain off and opened it to an empty hallway.

"Wow, you really just woke up, huh? I was being funny. Go and look at the links I sent you earlier."

"Links?" Nate closed the door and sighed. "What links?" He switched Charlie to speaker and looked at the screen. Charlie had messaged him with about a million links.

"Yeah. So you're officially on the Fairyland social media circuit," Charlie said.

"What? I am?"

"You are. Welcome to the circus, my friend! By the way, you're useless until you've woken up properly, so sort yourself out. Call me later and we can get dinner or something, okay?" Charlie was laughing at him, but Nate didn't particularly care.

"Yeah, sounds good. Thanks, Charlie."

Nate wandered to the kitchen and looked in his fridge. He had a half bottle of orange juice and some dubiously aged bagels. He pulled them out, took a swig from the juice bottle and chewed on the top bagel. It would have been better toasted but, eh, effort.

He took his breakfast to the living room and sat on the couch to look at the links Charlie had sent.

The first was an Instagram post, one of the guests Nate had met in the morning the day before – a woman in her twenties in a Fairyland tank top and cut-off jean shorts. He vaguely remembered her. She'd posted a shot of them posing together that Simon had taken with her phone. She'd captioned it: *Look who's back and more handsome than ever! #PrinceValor #MyHero #FairyLandMagic*

He wasn't supposed to announce to anyone on social media that he was Valor, but he liked the post anyway and clicked through to the woman's profile. She was a big Fairyland fan, often posting images from her visits to the park.

The other links Charlie had sent him were similar – lots of fans, Nate posing with children or with Ariana. He liked the one of him spinning the kid in the princess dress, they were both laughing and the photographer had caught the blue sky behind them.

There was a particularly lovely group shot with Greer, Ari, Dashiel, and Nate together.

They all looked so happy. He smiled looking at it.

I look like I belong there.

The thought filled him with the sensation of lightness. A weight lifted off him. *Like I've completed some kind of quest, maybe? Is this what Charlie had meant when he said I'd "arrived"?*

Nate sat back, holding his phone in the air as he leaned his head back on the couch and clicked through the links, and then once Charlie's fan links ran out, he browsed the sites to read more about what fans were saying about Fairyland.

Then he found himself clicking on Prince Justice hashtags.

There were so many photos and reposts, people absolutely gushing over him. He couldn't help but smile – seeing how people responded to Dashiel was both heartwarming and humbling.

He'd already known this job was important, personally, but for the first time it truly sank in for him that his performance as Valor mattered to hundreds of people. *Thousands.*

Maybe even more?

And Dashiel had been right. It was obvious that he knew what he was doing. Nate sighed. He should definitely pay attention to what Dashiel had to say.

He saved a couple of fan photos of himself and sent them through to his mother, already knowing that she'd burst with pride when she opened them.

The rest of the weekend stretched out before him. He ordered a pizza and some sides for delivery and put on the Princess Patience movie. May as well research as he relaxed.

As the familiar music started up he thought again about Dashiel. There was no point pretending that they were going to be friends, but he hoped Dashiel would continue to mentor him. He was so freaking handsome, after all. And they'd had a couple of really good moments together. If only he could understand why Dashiel seemed to hate him, sometimes.

21 / DASH

DASH'S WEEKEND ROUTINE SELDOM CHANGED. WHEN HE HAD A friend staying, maybe, or if he got sick, but those were rare exceptions. His usual routine was always the same.

He slept in until eight, went to the gym for a longer version of his daily workout, and followed this up with yoga or some other stretch class.

After the gym, he'd go for a protein smoothie and something from the cabinet at the café down the road. It was a surfer-style place, with lots of organic tofu, free range eggs, and locally sourced apple juice. It wasn't exactly Dash's style, but the smoothies were delicious and the staff were friendly.

After brunch, he'd do his weekly food shopping at the farmer's market for the freshest fruit and vegetables. Then on to the nice local butcher for free range chicken and lean beef, and maybe the fish shop if they had any nice-looking cuts.

He'd carry his groceries home, unpack them, do a quick house clean: bathroom, kitchen, floors. Then the laundry, changing the sheets on his bed and dusting off his shelves.

Then it was time to relax. He'd sit at his dining table with his laptop and a cup of chamomile tea, opening up all the fan sites he kept an eye on and reading what people were saying about him. It usually took a couple of cups of tea to go through the Fairyland news. This week he felt a little nervous as the sites loaded. He felt a flutter of fear - what if people liked Nate more than they liked him? Or rather, if they liked Valor more than Justice?

He always skipped the Prince Magnificence and Prince Diligence posts, and there hadn't been any Valor posts for months. With Nate on the job as Valor for only one day this week, there weren't as many posts about Valor as there were about Prince Justice.

But people were excited about the new prince all the same. His heart sped up a little.

That was always going to happen, he told himself. *It doesn't mean no one likes you anymore. Justice. People still like Justice.*

He looked through each one, paying careful attention to the captions and the close-up pictures people had taken of Nate as Prince Valor.

He's so handsome. Like the cartoon character come to life, ready to charm the socks off anyone who came near him. And his lips are so full and soft. And his eyes are gorgeous and... Dash took a breath shaking his head vigorously.

Stop it, Dash. Don't be an idiot.

He saved a couple of shots of the group of them. There was a particularly well-composed group shot that he convinced himself he wanted to show Greer.

And that's the only reason I'm saving them. To show Greer. Not so I'll have them on my phone for future reference.

Dash cleared his throat and took another sip of tea. Once he'd read all he wanted to, he moved to the couch and put the Princess Honesty movie on, got out his binder of Prince Justice character notes and read through them as the movie played. After that, he loaded up the Christmas television special that had all of the princes and princesses together. He paid special attention to the times Justice and Valor interacted and made some new notes.

This isn't personal, he thought. *It's not about Nate and me. It's about who's the better prince: Justice or Valor. And I'm going to ensure everyone knows it's Justice. No matter how much his eyes sparkle or how photogenic that smile is. I'm fucking photogenic, too and I am going to prove it.*

22 /NATE

AFTER A RELAXING SUNDAY OF DOING LAUNDRY AND NAPPING, NATE felt rested and ready for a full week of Valor-ing.

He said good morning to everyone he encountered on the way into the park, through the park, to the airlock and in the character changing rooms. Cody fist-bumped him as he came through the door.

"Morning, Cody."

"Morning, Nate. Good weekend?" Cody asked.

"Yeah, really chill," he said. "How about you?"

He shrugged one shoulder. "Same old stuff I always do."

Nate stopped before heading into the changing room. He looked at Cody over his shoulder. "Can I ask you a question?"

"Sure, shoot." Cody nodded for Nate to continue.

"Why are you here? I mean, I feel like you could probably walk into any security job you wanted. Why did you choose Fairyland?"

Cody gave Nate a slight smile. After a brief pause, he answered. "Even veterans with prosthetic limbs want to believe in magic, I guess."

Nate tried not to double take at the mention of a prosthetic limb. He hadn't noticed anything about Cody, which meant it was

109

probably one of or part of his legs. It didn't matter though, if Cody could work as a security guard, he must be managing it well. It also explained why he was working here and not still serving. Cody was eyeing him, and Nate recognized the look - he was waiting to see how Nate would react to his admission.

Kinda like coming out as gay, Nate thought.

Nate smiled and reached to give him another fist bump. "Good answer, man."

Cody grinned and returned it, giving him a little nod. "Best of luck out there today."

Monday was busy. One meet and greet in the morning, the parade, then two meet and greets in the afternoon when the park was busier. In between, Nate made sure to eat and hydrate, refilling his water bottle a couple of times.

"Careful of drinking too much," Dashiel said. It was just before the parade, and Nate set his bottle straight down. "Remember there's no pee breaks once we're out there."

"Yeah, I know," Nate smiled. Ever since his incident as Treasure, it really felt like Dashiel was trying to be his friend. And that felt good. Like a relief.

"Fine line, right? Too little and I'll go loopy, too much and things get uncomfortable."

"A fine line, indeed," Dashiel nodded. He stood up from his station, glanced at the mirror and nodded to Nate. "Ready for the parade?"

"Mmhmm." Nate stood up and patted his costume down. Everything was in place.

At the morning meet and greet Nate and Dashiel had been playing off each other again, but it was at the afternoon's first meet and greet that Nate noticed Dashiel was being sort of... extra.

For each new guest who approached he would do something different – a bow, a high five, or he would take their hand and lead them elegantly towards Greer. They were at the castle, so sometimes he'd gesture to that and make some joke about guests staying in their spare rooms or something.

It was charming, and the guests ate it up. Lennon and Neve had arranged the pairs so guests met Princess Patience and Prince Valor first and then moved to Justice and Honesty before leaving down the path.

Nate and Ari were having a great time together, but it became harder and harder to ignore the excitement Dashiel was creating. The delighted laughter and raised voices of the guests as they joked with Justice, Simon directing people to pose with them, and Greer's musical laughter carrying over the conversations Nate and Ari had with guests. Nate tried to do his best to focus on being the best Valor he could, but Dashiel was distracting.

"I'm so glad you're back!" A young man approached Nate and Ari. He was probably only a year or two younger than him. He wore a rainbow Fairyland T-shirt with the sleeves cut off, probably to show off his well-toned biceps and shoulders. Nate dragged his attention off Dashiel to smile at him.

"I'm glad to be back," he said. "What's your name?"

"Lief," he said. He waved another young man over who was hanging back, taking photos with his phone. "And this is my boyfriend, Mac."

Nate smiled extra wide and took Ari's arm. "It's good to meet you both. I'm sure you've heard of my beloved, Princess Patience?"

Lief and Mac smiled at her, and Lief even bowed a little.

"A pleasure. May we have a photo with you two?"

"Of course," Ari bobbed a little curtsey. "What a handsome couple you make."

Nate glanced at her, pleased but unsure for a second. Were they really allowed to say stuff like that to gay people? The policies on acknowledging things like divorced parents or recent deaths were pretty clear but did being gay gel with the park's traditional values? Nate corrected his posture, standing a little straighter.

Well, it shouldn't be a problem as long as we're delivering Fairyland magic, right? Why would it matter what the orientation of the guests is? Besides, part of the reason I took this role was to show that all people should be accepted. These guys are just like me, and I want them to have a great day.

"Thank you," Mac said to Ari. Lief moved so that he was in front of them and reached for one of Mac's hands. He glanced towards Simon, who was there, snapping photos.

"Mac, I love you," he said, raising his voice and turning toward Mac. He sank to one knee. Nate saw Mac's eyes widen and go shiny with tears. He even seemed to stop breathing.

Next to Nate, Ari gasped, and her hand flew up to her mouth. Nate's heart pounded with excitement. He tried to compose himself but he was so surprised he was sure he was just standing there with his mouth wide open.

"Will you make me the happiest prince in Fairyland and marry me?" Lief asked, his voice catching. Tears spilled over, running down Mac's cheeks as he nodded. Lief produced a ring from his pocket and they fumbled for a moment to get it on Mac's finger.

It all happened in a few seconds, but Simon was there, moving in closer to capture the moment, grinning broadly. Lief stood up and Mac wrapped his arms around him. They kissed deeply.

Dashiel patted Lief on the back when they were done – Nate wasn't even sure when he'd come over to this side of the alcove.

"Congratulations, good sir!" he said, turning to Mac to say the same.

"Thanks, Prince Justice," Lief smiled, his cheeks flushed and his eyes sparkling.

Nate moved forward, an anxious fluttering in his gut, feeling like he hadn't been quick enough off the mark if Dashiel had got there first. He congratulated them both and Simon insisted on some group shots with the happy couple. The waiting queue applauded, a few wiping their eyes.

As Lief and Mac moved off, Dashiel raised his voice. "Let us all celebrate, for these two honorable gentlemen are going to dedicate their lives to each other, and they will live happily in love forever!"

The queue broke into cheers and enthusiastic applause. Simon gave Mac a token for the photos and Lief beamed as they left.

Nate looked at Dashiel. While he realized he'd kind of saved Nate again because he'd been hesitating, there was something about the interaction that made him feel uncomfortable.

"Thank you," Nate said, his voice low. Dashiel nodded and he and Greer went back to their positions for the next lot of guests.

At the end of the day, Nate changed out of his costume and went to find Charlie at the Forest Kitchen.

The Forest Kitchen was a decorated restaurant made to look like you were eating with forest animals – if forest animals ate diner-style with someone cooking for them. The booths were designed to look like bushes and trees, the walls were covered with leaves and branches which protruded here and there, and there were little animatronic birds in the branches which would tweet or flap their wings.

Nate went to the front counter, his staff lanyard around his neck. The girl at the counter's nametag read 'Nova'.

"Hey Nova. Is Charlie Carson done for the day?"

"Another half hour. We had someone not turn up today, so he's covering shift change," she said.

"No worries. Can I get a woodland muffin special while I wait, please?"

Nate went to a corner booth with his wooden table marker and waited. When it was delivered, the special turned out to be a chocolate and raspberry muffin, a little bowl of carrot and celery sticks and an orange juice. He steadfastly ignored the vegetables, cut his muffin open and spread it generously with butter.

Charlie emerged after about a half hour and sat down on the other side of the booth, a large to-go cup of something in his hand.

"You haven't eaten your carrots," he tutted.

Nate shrugged. "Don't like them."

Charlie shook his head. "You know, someday you'll be older and your body will have to deal with all this crap you eat. And then you'll be all like, 'Charlie, why am I so sick all the time?'"

Nate grinned. "Yeah, but that's years away."

"Uh-huh, sure. You're hopeless." Charlie helped himself to the carrot sticks. "How'd your day go?"

"Really good, this couple got engaged in our meet and greet. A gay couple, too. It was really sweet."

Charlie's face lit up. He took a handful of carrot and celery. "That sounds amazing. Come on, let's get going. If I have to listen to the 'Forest Kitchen Ambience' playlist one more time I'm gonna lose it."

They walked to the staff car park and Nate told him all the details of Lief and Mac's engagement. When they got in the car, Charlie was silent for a moment. Nate's stomach dropped as he looked at him.

"What's happening? You didn't start the car."

"So… they came to you and got engaged?"

"Yeah. That's what I said."

"And then Prince Justice moved in and took over the moment? Dashiel made it all about him?"

Nate swallowed. He'd been dreading that his hunch about Dashiel had been right. "I mean, kind of? But I sort of froze. I didn't know how to react. It was good he stepped in." Nate bit his lip.

"But they came to you – to Prince Valor. They clearly like Valor better." Charlie started the car and pulled out of the car park.

"Does it really matter? They were so happy, it was a nice moment."

Charlie frowned. "I wonder why he made it about him, is all." He tapped his fingers against the steering wheel. "I mean, a guy like that... What does he have to gain by upstaging you?"

Nate felt a sinking feeling in his chest. Although he'd tried to give Dashiel the benefit of the doubt, he *had* been extra all day. What could have possibly made him change? Was he feeling threatened by Nate, or was something more nefarious going on?

What did Nate have that Dashiel would want? He crossed his arms over his chest as he racked his brain.

"Shit. The parade," he breathed.

It had to be what Dashiel was going after, it made the most sense.

How could he have thought that Dashiel liked him? That he was a friend? All if it – the friendship and everything – it was all a ruse so Nate would fail at getting the float. But what did he have to gain from that? Besides, they were all meant to be working together as a team, weren't they?

He couldn't imagine Lennon intentionally setting Dashiel and Nate against each other. But maybe Dashiel was focused on pushing his own career forward.

And to think, earlier today Nate had imagined what it would feel like to kiss him again.

"Wait... You mean you think he's trying to out-prince you?" Charlie asked.

Nate gritted his teeth as betrayal flared hot through his veins, quickly turning to white hot anger. "Let him fucking try."

23 /DASH

Dash got to the park early on Tuesday to be absolutely sure he was well prepared for the first meet and greet. He went to Wardrobe to find Molly already there, pinning a new Princess Constance dress on a dress form, half made. She looked over at him with an arched eyebrow.

"Hey Dash, you split your pants?"

"No, I was just wondering, are there any planned upgrades to my costume?" He asked idly, like he was just dropping in in case there were updates to be made.

Molly shook her head. "You know the drill, no upgrades unless there's a special occasion. And before you try and spin something, special occasions are park-sanctioned events like Christmas – not because you're bored."

Dash cleared his throat and went to touch the single sleeve hanging on the Constance dress. The fabric was a thick, smooth yellow satin. "Yeah, I know. But if, for example, I wanted to add a cape or something?"

Molly rolled her eyes. "You want to be Superman now?"

"No. Yes. Not Superman, but a bit more impressive, maybe," Dash said.

Molly narrowed her eyes suspiciously. "I don't know what

you're up to, Dash, but whatever. Run it past Central Design, get a sketch approved by the Look Specialists and I'll start making you a fucking cape."

Dash kicked the ground, feeling like a kid asking for candy from some relative who didn't want to spoil him. "How about new boots?"

"You had new boots three months ago. You can't possibly have worn them out already."

Dash's heart sank. He knew it'd be a long shot to get something added to his costume, but he had hoped Molly would do it for him anyway.

Just to get a little edge on the shiny new Prince Valor.

"No, no. They haven't worn out." He shoved his hands in his pockets.

Molly stared at him with her eyebrows raised and her lips pursed. She sighed and turned back to the dress. She picked up her pins. Dash sighed. He was wasting her time, they both knew it. But he had to try everything to make this work.

"What if I just put some trim on–"

"No," Molly cut in.

"Just a little, around the shirt collar?"

"We're done," Molly said to the dress, sticking it more violently than needed with a pin. "Have a nice day, Dash."

He knew not to argue with her, so he said goodbye and left Wardrobe. Next, he headed into the Princess's changing room to find Greer. She was half made up, reading a paperback crime thriller. Her hair was a mess and she was still in the comfy workout gear that she wore most mornings.

"Morning," he said. He sat down next to her.

"Mornin', Dash," she said. "Just let me finish this chapter."

Dash waited a full minute, but he couldn't get his brain to stop whirring. He launched into telling Greer about the ideas he'd had overnight.

117

"What if, when a couple comes to see us, I ask the girl to dance and you ask the guy."

"I think that'd be fine, assuming they're straight," she said, still reading. He frowned and then shook his head, undeterred.

"How about a new story we could tell people like we adopted a puppy together. It could be a stray puppy that we rescued from an evil wizard or something."

"They'd ask to see the puppy."

"Right. Do you think a kitten is better, then? We could say she's shy of strangers, so we can't bring her out to meetings."

Greer sighed and put her book down, marking her place with a hairpin. She gave him a look. "We could also say we started an ostrich ranch and took in refugees from the witch war crisis, but what's the point?"

Dash frowned, running his fingers through his hair. "No, we have to be more charming than that," He picked up her Fairyland regulation princess lipstick and fiddled with it, opening and closing the lid.

"I think you're missing my point spectacularly." She picked the lipstick off him and applied it, turning away from him to look at herself in the mirror.

"What if, on the walk to the meet up, we had a little scene. Like you could trip on your skirt and I catch you and you could say: 'Prince Justice, you're my hero'?"

"And what if I don't?" Greer snapped her lipstick closed.

"Yeah, but it'd be cute."

"Princess Honesty doesn't trip on her dress, she wears it all the time."

"Greer, this is serious. We have to up our game. Yesterday was good, but did you see Nate?" Dash reached for Greer's compact and she slapped his hand away. She rolled her eyes at him in exactly the same way Molly had.

"Yes. I saw Nate, he was fine."

"He was *better* than fine, he made it all look easy," Dash said.

He could hear himself getting louder and tried to modulate his volume a bit. "We need to plan something now so when it happens, *I* make it look easy."

"Okay, you're sounding a little crazy now," Greer said.

"I'm not crazy. I'm being smart, planning ahead."

She pushed an unopened water bottle towards him. "Have you eaten? I have a couple protein bars."

"I had steel cut oats with blueberries at home," he said, ignoring her jibe. "What about if a kid gives me something to sign, I could bow and then hand it to you like it's a precious gift?"

"You do that already," she said.

"I do?"

"Yes, and very naturally, like it's not even planned."

"Nate was wonderful with that little girl that had a cast on her leg the other day. Maia." He took the water bottle and opened it up, taking a drink and drumming his fingers on the counter.

"You're great with kids too," Greer said, absently.

"The empathy he showed, agreeing that he'd been afraid to get on his horse again? It was really good. Maybe I should modify my walk? He did a little bounce thing, it's hard to explain. It made his hair move in a really nice way. I wonder if I could do that, too."

"Oh my God," Greer said. "You're all over the place."

He ignored her. He was on a roll now.

"And when Leif proposed yesterday Nate looked so genuinely surprised and happy for them."

"Yes. Because *he was.*"

"But like, how could I look as natural as that? I could see the signs a mile away that the proposal was coming. It's happened so many times before. But Nate was just so much more in the moment. That's what's so good about his performance out there. He's *there*, you know?"

"Dash!" Greer said, loudly.

"What?"

"Can you hear yourself? You're full on obsessed with Nate!"

119

Greer stood, putting her hands on her hips, she glared down at him like she was scolding him. Which, she sort of was, he supposed.

Dash blinked at her and folded his arms tightly over his chest. "Look around you, Greer. Everyone is obsessed with Nate!"

"Dash, you're delusional," she said. She shook her head and turned to the mirror, sitting back down and picking up a makeup brush. "Go unwind before we have to go out there."

"It's true, though," he said, as he stood up. "The new Valor float, that one session as Treasure, hardly any training before being put out there in public, the social media, should I go on?"

"No, you should go stick your head in a bucket of water," Greer said. "You need to wake the hell up."

Dash stormed out of the room, barely stopping himself from slamming the changing room door. He knew he was right. He was totally justified in watching Nate's every move. The guy was some kind of mutant – no one was universally beloved by their workmates within a day.

I'm not obsessed, I'm being smart. I'm protecting myself. It's completely reasonable.

He went into the prince's changing room and saw Nate, he'd got distracted halfway through getting changed. Dash could tell because he had on his Valor pants but was half out of a soft looking grey flannel shirt. He was utterly focused on his phone, which meant Dash could stare at the muscles of his biceps and the lean angles of his waist and stomach. He swallowed and looked away.

It's not about that. It's not about him at all. It's about me showing how my years of experience make me the better prince, and I'm going to show him exactly that.

24 /DASH

Tuesday went well, despite Dash feeling a little off after Greer's accusations. There were no big moments during guest encounters the way they'd had on Monday. Nate and Ari mostly stayed on their side of the meet and greet spaces, and Dash and Greer kept doing just a little bit more for the people who came by.

On Wednesday, however, Dash woke up several times in the night.

Something was bothering him. He kept dreaming things which he woke up from with a startle - like he was running and he'd trip, or he'd open a door and someone would lunge at him. Each time he'd have to wait for his heart to slow down and his breathing to get to normal before he could drift back to sleep.

Maybe I'm putting too much pressure on myself, he thought. *But if anything is worth putting effort into, it's this job.*

To compensate for the lack of sleep, he drank far too much coffee. He was a bit on edge as a result –even more so than he'd already been.

It didn't matter though, the days of practicing being a bit better had kicked into muscle memory. His morning meet and greets with Greer went well, and the parade was one of their best yet.

But the afternoon meet and greet at the Reflecting Lake got a bit rowdy. The crowds were heavy for a Wednesday and there were a bunch of high school kids from out of State who were on some kind of field trip. They were all over the park in groups, getting over excited and making lots of noise.

The queue to see the princes and princesses was huge. Neve and Lennon were moving at double speed, organizing them and trying to keep the order.

At one point, maybe twenty minutes into the session, he recognized the little girl Nate had coaxed forward on his first day as a handler. Minako, and her father.

The father saw him looking as they got to the front of the queue and waved at him. Minako looked like she'd gone shy again, clinging to his leg and half hiding her face so that Dash could see the hem of her skirt sticking out and some straight black hair.

As she hesitated, and her father bent down a little to encourage Minako forward, the teens behind them got impatient.

"Aww, come on!" A teenage boy called out. He had a heavy black fringe combed forward over his face and was dressed in a black and white striped shirt and ripped black jeans. He folded his arms dramatically over his chest.

"Oh, feel free to go on ahead," Minako's father said. But just as he said it, Greer swept forward and opened her arms to the little girl.

"It's the Lady Minako! I'm so happy to see you again! How was your trip back?"

Minako smiled and ran forward, launching herself into Greer's arms.

The teens behind them moved forward, obviously having heard only Minako's father's encouragement and not paying attention otherwise. Dash held up a hand, asking them wordlessly to wait a moment, but they didn't seem to notice him.

Neve was talking to Simon, helping him with a camera jam or

something. Lennon was distracted with the guests who'd just been talking to Nate and Ari, showing them something on a paper map of Fairyland. Dash didn't know what to do, but he decided that if he focused on the little girl the teens would get the hint and wait, surely.

He knelt on one knee and Minako hugged him instantly. "Welcome back, Lady Minako," he said. "How has your week been?"

"Good!" she said, then looked back at the line. "Where's Nate? I thought he'd be here."

Dash looked over to where Nate was standing in full Valor costume before he could stop himself. Minako didn't notice, thankfully.

"He's uh, he's working at a different part of the park today," he said. "You might not see him."

"Is that Prince Valor?" Minako asked, pointing at Nate, her eyes wide.

Before Dash could reply, they were interrupted.

"Our turn," the teen with the swept-forward fringe said.

"Yes, that's Valor, he came back from his travels, far, far away," Greer said. "Are you excited to meet him?"

"Mmm," Minako nodded. She took hold of Dash's sleeve with one tight fist.

"Shall I take you over and introduce you?" Dash asked. Minako nodded again and he stood up.

"Well, *finally*," one of the teen girls said. The teens crowded in around Dash and Greer, getting in between them pushing them back towards the lake to take selfies. Dash took Minako's little hand and led her back from the crowd, towards Ari and Nate.

"Excuse me," Dash said, trying to keep the Prince Justice charm, even though by this stage he was fuming at the callousness of the teens. How could they not see that Minako needed a little extra time and space?

He tugged Minako towards the lake, using the paved edging

there as a passage to Nate and Ari. One teen in a fluffy pink skirt stepped back, trying to pull Greer into a pose with her, and collided with Minako. Minako lost her footing on the edge of the paved platform.

For a moment time slowed down as she toppled, arms windmilling, almost able to right herself before she fell into the lake with a splash.

Dash froze, his heart in his mouth.

What should he do?

The lake wasn't shallow at this end, so he couldn't wade in, and his costume was so cumbersome when it was wet – it would likely suck him under the water faster than Minako… then he'd be no use to either of them. He wasn't a strong swimmer.

Then there was a blur of blue and white and another splash.

After a moment of stunned silence, everyone started shouting at once.

"What happened?"

"Where's my daughter?"

"Oh my God!"

Nate surfaced out of the lake, an arm around the sodden Minako, who was clinging to him with both arms around his neck. Nate struck out towards the shore with one arm. Lennon rushed forward, guiding him to the emergency access at the side of the platform, where a ramp was hidden under the drooping leaves of a willow tree.

Nate's hair was ruined. His costume probably destroyed. The sleeves clung to his arms, showing off every curve of muscle.

Minako was crying, coughing and spluttering water out.

The teens around Dash all had their phones out, filming and taking pictures with their mouths wide open.

"I'm so sorry," the teen in the fluffy skirt cried. "I didn't see her, oh my god, I'm sorry!"

Dash looked for Greer, who moved gracefully to his side and took his arm.

"That was probably your big moment to be a hero," Greer said in that barely audible whisper they'd developed for each other.

Dash shook his head, unable to even process what had just happened.

"It's all right, she's fine," Neve said. She hovered nearby as Nate handed Minako to her father.

"Thank you, really," he said. "I was too far back, taking photos."

"Don't worry about it," Nate said. "It was nothing." He had a hand on Minako's back, his concern for her obvious, even though she was now out of danger.

The teens all started clapping, a couple of them making sighing noises but in the swoony, appreciative way.

Nate looked over and smiled and then he looked down in a self-deprecating way and raised a hand to wave at them.

He should have looked like a drowned rat, but he was holding himself with confidence. He kept looking back at Minako, his eyes shiny with concern.

He really cares about people, Dash thought. *It's not an act, any of it. He's just like this.*

"Come on, Prince Valor, let's get you a towel," Lennon said, patting Nate on the back.

The fluffy skirted teen rushed forward to Minako and her father. Minako had stopped coughing now, her fist balled in her father's shirt as he held her. She eyed the girl with deep suspicion.

"I'm so, so sorry. Please, let me buy you lunch, or a new dress, or a fluffy toy or something, anything. Please. I feel awful." The teen wiped away a tear.

Minako's father seemed to straighten his shoulders a little. "Be more careful in future," he said.

"Of course I will," she said. "Please, just let me get her something to say sorry."

He shook his head, but the teen followed as he walked off and

Dash suspected there'd at least be a plushie Treasure toy in Minako's future.

The rest of the teens split into two groups, one following Minako and another taking more photos of the soaked Nate, who was hurried off by Lennon, Ariana trailing behind, fawning over her handsome, heroic prince.

Neve hustled Greer and Dash back into position, a bit further away from the edge of the platform than they had been.

"Well that was certainly some excitement, lucky our dashing Prince Valor was here to save that little girl," Neve said, loudly, performing a little for the people still in the queue. "But, Princess Honesty and Prince Justice, we still have some lovely guests to meet."

"Of course, let's not keep them waiting," Dash lowered his head in acknowledgement, but his heart was thumping and his stomach hurt.

He'd been so worried about how he'd look that he had frozen. He'd been petrified for Minako but he couldn't take action to save the little girl, and he'd been the closest to her.

He'd got himself so wrapped up in the idea of being better than Nate, that he'd hesitated – and risked someone's life in the process.

His hands shook as he clenched them behind his back. He'd lost sight of the whole reason he loved this job. It wasn't because of a float in the parade, or because he got the most likes on Instagram. It was because he wanted to make the experience magical. He wanted to make the world a slightly better place.

And instead, when it came down to it, he'd been all show and no substance.

He shook his head and focused on the next group of teens, giving them a wide smile that didn't reach his rattled heart.

"How lovely to meet you, what are your names?" he said, swallowing his turbulent emotions and looking each of them in the eye.

25 /NATE

Lennon took Nate to the showers in the back of the Wardrobe building.

"Usually the fursuit people use these. As you're aware, they get very hot," they said.

"Thanks, Lennon." Nate went into the cubicle and sighed as he stripped off the wet costume.

Dashiel had looked rattled when Nate had emerged from the lake. Like, truly shaken. All day he'd been doing his Uber Prince Justice thing, being extra great. And then when someone had needed him the most, he'd frozen, and Nate had out-princed him without even thinking.

Not that he would have done anything else. Minako was in trouble and he was a strong swimmer. Still, he felt embarrassed about how extra he must've looked, diving in like that. And of course all those teenagers had been taking photos. They were probably already online. With his luck, the whole moment would be overblown to complete ridiculousness.

Nate flicked his damp hair out of his eyes and then leaned back into the shower spray, letting it warm him. He should apologize to Dashiel. Talk to him about the whole competition thing Dashiel seemed to think they were in. It was all so unnecessary, especially when anyone could see they were better when they worked together and played off each other.

Yeah. He'd track down Dashiel and apologize. He'd suggest they could be friends, or at least coworkers who supported each other rather than tried to outdo each other.

Nate stepped out of the shower and picked up a towel. He groaned when he realised that he hadn't brought anything to change into.

"Um, hello?" He called out. "Lennon? Ari? Anyone?"

He heard footsteps. "Nate?" Teddy called back. "You okay in there, Superman?"

"Um... no, I didn't bring any dry clothes," Nate said. "Could you get my workout gear for me, please?"

Teddy chuckled from the other side of the cubicle door. "Take mine," he said. "It'll be quicker. I'll be right back – just have to get them from my locker."

A couple of minutes later and Teddy was back and knocking on the door.

"Is that you?"

"Yeah, open up, I got clothes for you, clean and dry."

Nate opened the door, a towel around his waist, feeling sheepish. "Thanks, man."

"Anything for the hero of the hour," Teddy winked. He broke into a huge grin.

"Don't call me that. It makes me uncomfortable." Nate took the clothes and got dressed as quick as he could. Teddy's clothes were only a couple of sizes too big. Teddy chuckled when Nate emerged.

"Don't worry little buddy, you'll grow into them someday," he teased. He plucked at the loose sleeve of the t-shirt he'd loaned him.

Nate laughed. "Thanks, I think?" He picked up his wet costume and handed it to Teddy, who folded it over a spare towel so it wouldn't drip everywhere. "I assume you're going to deal with that?'

"Yep. You're pretty much done for the day, right?" Teddy asked, walking with Nate through Wardrobe.

"Yeah, that was my last meet and greet, unless Lennon has a different idea."

"So that must mean you have time to tell me exactly what happened out there." Teddy hopped from foot to foot, a strangely comic movement for such a tall, broad shouldered man. "The rumors are off the scale of credibility."

"It wasn't too much," Nate shifted uncomfortably and looked towards the door which led to the prince's changing room.

"Pleeease?" Teddy pleaded, his face equal parts hopeful and expectant.

Nate didn't want to disappoint him. "Well, some teens were being pushy, and they crowded Dashiel and Greer while they were still with this little girl. And then she lost her footing when someone bumped into her, and she fell into the water. Right into the lake."

"And then?" Molly asked. She must've overheard them and got curious, Nate hadn't even seen her approach.

Nate noticed that the Wardrobe sewing machines had fallen silent. Everyone in the vicinity was listening, but pretending not to be. He sighed and raised his voice so they didn't have to pretend.

"And then I jumped in," He shrugged. "Because she was like, four years old and wearing a big fluffy princess dress."

"You just jumped in? *That* was your first instinct rather than call for help, or like, scream or whatever?" Molly asked.

"I was a surf lifesaver in high school," Nate said. He rubbed the back of his head, feeling very conspicuous with everyone hanging off his words.

"You're a real-life hero," Teddy said, shaking his head in awe.

"It was just reacting. I didn't even think," Nate said.

"Well that just makes you *more* of a true hero." Molly handed him a cup of steaming tea. "Jumping into action to save those in need." Then she smiled while tilting her head and fluttering her eyelashes at him, sighing in imitation of how Princess Patience did in the movie.

"Yeah, soooo, uh... that's what happened. Can I go now?" Nate's insides squirmed, he wanted to get away to speak to Dashiel before he left for the day.

"Fine. But give me your number so if I trip over on the way home, I can call you to come catch me," Teddy overexaggerated a swoon.

"No, give your number to *me*," Molly said. "If I encounter a puddle, I might need you to lay your cape over it."

Nate scrunched his nose and pointed a finger at them. "None of you get my number," he said. He laughed, more comfortable with them teasing him than the praise. Teasing, he could deal with.

"Aw come on!" Molly pouted.

Nate lifted his nose in the air. "Only royalty is worthy of my number!" He huffed and flounced out of Wardrobe, doing an exaggerated version of Dashiel's Prince Justice walk. The sounds of them all laughing made him laugh, too. Yes, that was much easier to cope with than adulation.

Nate went straight into the Prince's changing room, but Dashiel had already gone. The room was quiet – except for Tristan, who was half in his Sparkles the Friendly Dragon costume.

"Hey, it's the hero of the day!"

"Everyone knows, huh?"

"It's practically being shouted from the rooftops." Tristan laughed as Nate went to his locker to get his things. "I mean, in a good way though, don't stress about it, man."

"Is that Nate?" Lennon poked their head into the changing room. "How're you doing?"

Nate looked over, pocketing his wallet and keys and checking his phone. "I'm good, aside from of the entirety of Wardrobe making fun of me."

Lennon frowned. "Those clothes look way too big for you."

"Yeah, they're Teddy's." Nate looked at his regular clothes in his locker and shut the door. He didn't want to waste more time, he wanted to talk to Dashiel before he left, if he could still catch him.

"Good work today. You really went above and beyond," Lennon said. "It's just the kind of thing we want to see during this trial period. Your actions, I mean – not the kid falling in the water. That was a disaster. They're putting in guardrails, so no meet and greets at the Lake for the next couple of days."

"Those teens were kind of out of control," Nate said, pulling on his grey denim jacket over Teddy's T-shirt. He waved to Tristan and walked over to Lennon, they were kind of blocking the way out.

"Yes, but that's on me. I'll be more attentive and call for Cody if we get that busy again." Lennon looked genuinely sorry. Nate smiled to show them he wasn't annoyed.

"Thanks." Nate hesitated for a moment. "Was Dashiel okay, after everything?"

Lennon cocked their head to the side but answered all the same. "He's fine, he said he had some stuff to do so he's gone already."

"Oh. Okay, um." Nate swallowed. "I wanted to talk to him, could you maybe give me his number?"

"I can't, I'm sorry. Employee confidentiality. You'll just have to wait for him to come in tomorrow." Lennon squeezed his shoulder with one hand. "You really did great today. I'm proud of you."

"Thanks, Lennon," Nate smiled. Then he turned back to the changing rooms, wondering what his next move should be. He really wanted to talk to Dashiel. Tonight.

Wait, Greer hangs out with him all the time, I'm sure she'd let me have his number.

He knocked on the Princess's changing room door.

Ari invited him in; she and Greer had changed already. Ari was in jeans and a loose-fitting Fairy Gentle T-shirt, whereas Greer was in a tight purple dress and heels.

"You headed out somewhere?" Nate asked.

"Mmm-hmm, hot date," Greer said. She was doing some last-minute touches on her going out makeup. It was quite different from the Princess Honesty makeup, more dramatic. "Well, I'm hoping. Who knows if people really look like the pictures they upload, right?"

"Right," Nate said. He moved nearer her station so he didn't have to raise his voice too much to ask this next bit. "Sorry to bug you like this, but I really wanted to talk to Dashiel. Today. And he's already gone."

"Mmm-hmm," she said again. She was concentrating on her eyeliner.

"And, well... I wondered if you'd mind giving me his number?" Nate asked. Asking it was awkward enough his skin crawled a little. Was he being unethical? Greer met his eyes in the mirror.

"I don't think he'd like that, Nate. Honestly."

Nate sighed and slumped into the chair beside her. "Yeah, I agree. But it's important, and I need to get it out before tomorrow." Greer looked at him for a long moment and then shrugged one shoulder.

"I'll check with him." Greer picked up her phone and texted at lightning speed.

Ari gave Nate a hug from behind, and as he half turned in the seat to hug her back, she gave him a kiss on the cheek. "See you tomorrow, my prince," she said, giving him a playful wink.

"Later, Ari, have a good night."

Greer's phone beeped and Nate's heart leapt into his throat.

"He says you can come around to his place," she said. "And, you know what? I think it's a good idea. He needs some sense talked into him, and he's not listening to me."

"Wait, he doesn't want me to have his number, but I can know where he lives?" Nate frowned.

"Yeah, go figure. He likes in-person chats, I guess. You got a ride?"

He shook his head.

"I can take you, it's not far from the place I'm meeting my date."

"Oh, you don't have to do that," Nate said. "I can get a cab or a rideshare or something." Charlie was on some kind of weird split shift, so he had bussed in that morning.

Greer packed her things into a small, sparkly clutch and stood up. "I know, but you've inspired me with your heroic actions and good deeds." Greer wiggled her eyebrows at him.

"No one's letting this go any time soon, are they?" Nate asked, rubbing a hand over his eyes like he could erase what'd happened at the lake and just go back to being regular Nate.

Greer popped a piece of pink bubble gum in her mouth and slipped an arm around Nate's shoulders, squeezing him against her. "Not on your nelly."

26 /NATE

GREER DROPPED NATE OFF AT DASHIEL'S BUILDING. IT WAS A NICE part of town, and although the building looked less nice than some of the others around, it was high enough on a rise that it would have an epic view.

Greer had given him the apartment number and driven off, wishing him good luck and laughing in a somewhat terrifying way.

Did she expect Nate to crash and burn, maybe? Or did she just like the idea that he was going to make Dashiel awkward?

Now that he was here, at the building, Nate second-guessed himself. Dashiel probably didn't ever want to see him again, Nate had shown him up and who wanted to talk to someone who'd done that?

And what was he gonna say, anyway? 'Sorry for saving a little girl?' or, 'I don't want a dragon float so you have nothing to fear from me'. But he *did* want a dragon float. It sounded so cool!

Maybe 'sorry for busting in and making you think you weren't good enough, even though you're totally amazing and hot and nice when you want to be'. Yeah, that'd go down really well. Just peachy. He rubbed his hand over his eyes and sucked in his breath.

He opened the rideshare app on his phone and then remembered that Dashiel was expecting him to show up. He couldn't back out now. Not without a brilliant excuse.

Nate bit his lip, put his phone in his jacket pocket and straightened his spine. He pushed his shoulders back and pressed the buzzer for Dashiel's apartment.

After a half minute, Dashiel's voice crackled down through the intercom.

"Hello?"

"Hey, it's Nate!" He instantly regretted sounding so upbeat – he was there to clear the air, not deliver a fancy meal from the local restaurant or whatever it was that rich people had delivered.

"Come on up," Dashiel said. There was a beeping noise and the doors opened.

Nate spent the elevator ride up trying not to hyperventilate as he over thought what he was doing there. Why had he thought this was a good idea? This was going to be *terrible*. Dashiel was definitely going to yell at him. Or freeze him out. *Or maybe...*

Maybe he'd think this was some kind of terribly timed booty call?

Nate checked himself out in the mirrored surface of the elevator doors. He looked okay. Freaked, but okay. He was still wearing Teddy's clothes, and they were far too big. He tried running his hands through his hair to fluff it up in the front, but since the douse in the lake and the shower it was weird and flat. He tucked the front of the T-shirt into the waistband of the pants in case it made him look a little more put together.

The doors opened and he went out into an impeccable hallway. The floor was carpeted in pale grey, the walls were cream colored, and there were potted yucca plants dotted in between the dark grey doors. Each door was emblazoned with a shiny metal number.

Dashiel's door was slightly open, so Nate swallowed, knocked and walked in.

"Hello?"

"Through here," Dashiel called out. Nate followed his voice through the tidiest house Nate had ever seen. It was like one of those example show apartments they made to get people to invest in new buildings. Or like it'd just been professionally cleaned to be rented out as an Airbnb.

Dashiel was in the kitchen doing the washing up. He was dressed down, in track pants and a tank top. Nate could see all of his arms and it made his mouth go dry.

"Hey, Dash – Dashiel," Nate said. Dashiel turned to look at him. He raised his eyebrows.

"What are you wearing?"

"I borrowed Teddy's stuff," Nate said. He looked down at himself. "He's tall."

"That he is," Dashiel said. "So what brings you here? Greer said you wanted to talk."

Nate looked around, the two takeaway menus on the fridge were lined up perfectly with the top of the fridge door. The draining rack only had one plate, one saucepan and some cutlery on it. There was a bowl brimming with fresh fruit on the breakfast bar.

"Um, I wanted to talk," Nate said.

"Yeah, I got that," Dashiel said. He smiled and filled an electric kettle with water. "You want a cup of tea or coffee?"

"Coffee sounds great," Nate said, even though he didn't usually have caffeine after three. Dashiel busied himself with cups.

"I wanted to say sorry," Nate said. Dashiel paused and glanced at him over his shoulder before going back to his preparations.

"For what?"

"For freaking you out, I guess. I don't want you to feel like you have to do… more than usual."

Dashiel stopped mid-movement. "Oh," he said.

"I mean, you can't keep doing more than usual. You'll wear yourself out, exhaust yourself, and you don't need to."

"Ohh-kay? Sugar or creamer?"

"Yes, both thanks," Nate said. Dashiel kind of huffed like he'd expected Nate to be the kind of guy who took both sugar and creamer. Nate jumped in again. "Or black is fine."

Why was he trying so hard to please Dashiel all of a sudden? Or impress him?

"How many sugars?"

"Umm, two." Nate swallowed back his nervousness and tried again to explain himself. "The thing is that I didn't expect any of this when I started. I thought I'd be working as a handler and then as Treasure the Unicorn for a month at least. I didn't expect things to happen so fast."

"Well, that's not your fault." Dashiel handed Nate a stylish black mug with a silver Treasure outline on it.

"This is cute," Nate said. He held the mug up and looked at it.

"Staff discount, it was a nice range," Dashiel shrugged.

"Well, that aside. What do you think?" Nate's breathing was getting shallow, he was putting himself out there and Dashiel was barely responding to him. He wanted some kind of feedback from him.

Dashiel frowned. "What do I think about what?"

Nate wrapped his hands around the mug.

Why was Dashiel being so obtuse? So hard to get through to?

"About my apology? About… me?"

"I mean, it's fine. There's nothing to forgive ," Dashiel moved towards his living area and gestured for Nate to follow him. "I was actually thinking I owed *you* an apology."

Nate flopped down on the couch much faster than intended. His knees kind of gave out on him.

I'm too nervous for this. I should just leave.

Dashiel sat on the other end of the couch.

"You were thinking that?' Nate's voice broke a little.

For fuck's sake, get your voice under control, get it together, Nate told himself.

"Why'd your voice just do that?"

"No reason, just surprised, I guess." Nate fumbled with his Treasure cup, his clammy hands making the mug slippery. Miraculously it hadn't spilled when he'd more or less fallen on the couch.

Dashiel took a deep breath, looking into his cup of tea. "Look. I know I've been kind of a jerk." He looked up at Nate.

"No, you've done great, you've been really helpful training me." Nate shifted uncomfortably. It wasn't exactly the truth – not after how horrible Dashiel had been on his first day – but it wasn't a lie, either.

"Okay, but I also got pretty wrapped up in the idea of doing better than you." He sighed some, his jaw working. This was clearly costing him. Although he wanted to jump in, Nate stayed quiet, giving him time. "What you did today, jumping into the lake for that little girl?"

"Minako."

"Yeah, Minako. You kinda shook me up. Out of something. It was very quick thinking, I was impressed."

"Oh," Nate said. "But it was just instinct, because I used to do surf lifesaving in high school."

Dashiel sighed. He leaned back against the couch cushions and probably would have slumped except he still had great posture.

"Of course you did."

Nate prickled at the tone. "Why do people keep saying things like that? I just want to do my job. I wasn't trying to be a hero."

Nate hadn't realized how much that was bothering him until he said it out loud. He didn't want to be known for this, he wanted to be known for being a great Prince Valor, not just because he happened to have been a surf lifesaver. That was just a random thing from his past, and could just as easily have been something Dashiel had done and not Nate. Social Media was going to be flooded with him being a big hero, but he had just been the first person to react.

Dashiel moved a little closer to him. "But you did something heroic, you should get recognition for that."

Nate set his coffee down. It was still too hot to drink. He sighed and ran a hand through his hair. "I didn't come here so you could reassure me. I was meant to be reassuring *you*."

"But I don't really need reassurance from you. Not anymore."

Nate looked around the living room, chewing his lower lip. He couldn't see any family pictures, group photos with friends or really any evidence that Dashiel had people in his life at all.

"Okay, but you're getting reassurance from somewhere, right?"

Dashiel folded his arms over his chest, which Nate felt was an answer in and of itself. The silence stretched out until Nate couldn't stand it any longer.

"I don't mean to pry..." Nate trailed off.

"So, don't."

"But," Nate pressed on. "It seems like you're kind of... tightly wound. Do you ever do anything to blow off steam? Or like, talk to someone about your feelings."

Dashiel blinked at him. "That really has nothing to do with you. I barely know you."

"No, I know. And you don't have to tell me anything. It's just... it can be good to talk about stuff with someone. I know I'd be a total mess without Charlie."

"Who's Charlie?" Dash's eyes narrowed.

"My best friend, he referred me for the Fairyland job. He works in food service."

"Okay, so I should talk to Charlie?" Dashiel chuckled a little.

"No! I just mean... everyone needs someone to vent to, or just to go to when you feel like you've screwed up, or if you're unsure about something." Nate looked into Dashiel's face, this was all so awkward. "Is this sounding okay?"

"I have Greer," Dashiel shrugged. "She keeps me grounded."

"So, maybe she needs to tell you you're doing well? Do, do you need me to tell you that you're doing well?"

Dashiel licked his lips and shook his head. "To be honest, I don't even understand how we got onto this subject."

How had we got here? I came to say sorry, and I'd said this instead?

"I'm worried you don't have people to talk to. Is your family in the city?"

"My family died when I was a teenager," Dash cleared his throat and took a sip of tea.

Oh shit.

Nate picked up his cup again, trying to remember how to breathe. *I've totally overstepped. Maybe I should just leave? But then I've brought up this horrible memory and he's probably even more vulnerable. Got to try something else.*

"I'm sorry. I just think I'd like us to be friends. I'd like us to keep working together like we have been. Like when we were talking to Maia about her pony – that it was awesome."

"It was a good moment," Dashiel gave a him a half-hearted smile.

"And if you ever want to talk about...whatever with me, that's cool too. But no pressure, and I totally don't–" Nate stopped abruptly. He'd been about to bring up the kiss and tell Dashiel he wasn't expecting anything. Why? He dropped his gaze into his coffee cup, mortified.

"You don't what?" Dashiel asked.

"Nothing," Nate said. His voice cracked again.

"Come on, you can't just stop mid-sentence."

"Uhh, yes I can."

"You were just saying I should open up to someone more. That goes both ways. It sounded like you were about to say something pertinent."

"It wasn't. Um. You don't – I didn't want to bring up the kiss again. But now you kinda made me, so I was gonna say I totally don't want to kiss you, so you don't have to worry about it. That's not why I came here." Nate coughed.

He could totally tell that I was lying.

They were both silent for a second, the awkwardness between them sitting heavily like a third person on the couch. Nate sipped his coffee for something to do. Maybe Dashiel would pretend he hadn't brought the kiss up. Maybe he could teleport home if he concentrated on it hard enough.

"I'm sorry," Nate said. "I really didn't want to say all that. I know… I know you're not into it."

"It's not that I wasn't into it," Dashiel said. His voice was low enough that Nate had to lean in a little to hear it.

His lips looked so good. And the last kiss had been amazing. His eyes were so blue. His eyes. Was it my imagination or were Dashiel's eyes starting to close? He's leaned in, right? Was this happening again? Were they gonna make out?

I'll let this happen. I'll kiss the crap out of his face.

Dashiel shook his head and straightened up. "Well, I guess it's getting late."

"Uh, yeah, I guess?" Nate couldn't help but feel every second of the shiver of disappointment that snaked its way down his spine.

"I'll take that, don't worry about the cleanup," Dashiel took his cup off him and stood up. Nate hurried to stand up as well.

"Good talk, thanks for dropping by, Nate. I'll definitely take it under consideration."

He hurried Nate out, and it wasn't until he was the elevator heading back down that he had a moment to process what had just happened.

It'd felt like they were gonna kiss, right? He hadn't just imagined that. But then Dashiel had freaked and kicked him out.

Nate groaned, pressing his hot forehead against the cold, pristine mirror. It didn't cool his body down the way he needed it to.

Why had he gone and complicated his relationship with Dashiel all over again?

27 /DASH

DASH WOKE UP ON THURSDAY NUMB. WITH ALL THAT HAD HAPPENED the day - and evening - before, his brain had given up. He was just...done. He threw the covers off and sat up. He rubbed his face with one hand before getting up to brush his teeth.

He hadn't been able to settle to anything after he'd kicked Nate out. His mind had run in loops, distracting him from watching TV or a movie. He couldn't concentrate on reading the paper or the book he was reading. No, everything that was going through his mind, it was all Nate. Nate and the complicated whirl of emotions Nate brought up in him.

Nate telling him that he was doing well. Offering reassurance. Pointing out that maybe reassurance was something he needed more of in his life. Nate with both hands around his cup of coffee like he needed it to stay warm. Nate in a T-shirt far too large for him, the loose collar slipping down and exposing the line of his neck as it met his shoulder.

The way he had leaned in when Dash had nearly kissed him. Again.

He kept having these intense flashbacks to their initial kiss and how hot it'd been. The feel of Nate's hard body against his. The anger and passion. It made his mouth go dry.

Then he'd flash forward to Nate rescuing Minako and emerging from the lake with a white shirt soaked through, like he was the hero of some romantic drama.

Like he was the hero of one of Dash's rare romantic daydreams.

He felt a warm stirring at the thought of Nate as a romantic hero and then quelled it, gritting his teeth. He'd been brushing his teeth too long. He rinsed his mouth out, wiped the sink down and went to get dressed.

Yesterday, he had resolved to stop being a try hard and just do his job. And he'd decided to support Nate – however he needed it. Only, the resolution he'd felt yesterday was wavering.

In the kitchen, Dash brooded over the blending of his morning protein shake. The cup Nate had used was sitting on the draining rack, looking all innocent.

What had Nate even wanted, turning up at my house like that?

He looked at his phone, hoping for a distraction. Greer had texted to ask how things had gone with Nate. He texted back a brief brush off: *Fine. Cleared the air.*

He opened Instagram and the first thing he saw was Nate, emerging from the lake with his shirt soaked through like Mr Fucking Darcy, Minako clinging to his neck, his expression the inscrutable seriousness that Dash was unaccustomed to seeing on Nate's face.

A jolt went through him and his breath caught.

Absolutely gorgeous.

"Fuck," Dash breathed. He scrolled through the Fairyland fan accounts he followed, but it was all the same. Reports and reshares of Nate saving Minako. Hype about Prince Valor's triumphant return. The hashtags and comments were out of control: *#RealLifeHero #PrinceValorIsaHero #TrulyValorous!*

Dash sat at the dining table and sipped his smoothie without tasting it. He looked up the Fairyland fan sites and it was the same thing there. People sharing their descriptions – obviously, a couple of people had been there in the queue. There was even a video of Nate diving into the Reflecting Lake as Dash stood there with his mouth open.

Another video showed Nate handing Minako over to her father. Dash was there, off to the side in the background, standing there with mouth open, again.

Although a couple of people pointed out Justice's inaction and suggested he was being usurped, mostly he wasn't mentioned at all.

Which was worse? Dash thought. *Better to be thought of poorly than not thought of at all, right?*

The whole Fairyland internet community had devolved into a Prince Valor lovefest.

People were pledging their love, offering to marry him, planning trips to Fairyland just so they could meet him. A few joked that they'd fall into the lake on purpose just so he'd carry them back out. There were so many excited posts you'd have thought Nate had pulled the moon down and given it to Minako.

Nate, Nate, Nate. Dash had been right. Everyone was obsessed with Nate. Everyone.

He got up to clean out his smoothie glass, crashed it into the sink and realised he was angry and jealous again. He took a breath and checked the glass - no cracks.

Nate clearly didn't need his help, anyway. How do you coach someone who's an instant success? The fans love him, the whole park loves him. Dash wasn't needed. With a sinking sensation in his stomach, he gathered up his things and went to his car.

What if I'm not even relevant any more?

He made his way to work, still brooding. The morning was sunny and bright, but it couldn't reach Dash. He was in an angry, jealous bubble which stopped the sun warming him. He gritted his teeth until his jaw ached. His mind kept on whirling. One minute he was ready to coach Nate, the next he wanted to punch him. But he definitely couldn't kiss him again, even though that kept coming up too.

What was he going to do? If he did what he'd decided on and really mentored Nate, who knew what might happen between them? They just couldn't date, not if Dash wanted to keep his job.

He'd just have to make a little distance. While he helped him. Help, and take a step back. Because they couldn't be friends without being tempted to break the rules, that much was obvious.

This was of course, assuming Nate actually needed any help from Dash, which he doubted.

He switched off the car radio so he didn't have external noise as well as internal.

Nate's voice echoed in his head *"Do you need me to tell you that you're doing well?"*

Dash gripped the steering wheel harder, narrowing his eyes. What did Nate know about it? Dash was fine. He had Greer.

Besides, Dash was always busy with the gym, or work prep or research. It just didn't leave time for calling people or hanging out. He was used to being alone.

He sighed and unclenched his jaw, taking a deep breath. He was gripping the wheel so hard his knuckles were white, making the scar on his left hand extra obvious.

I have to calm down, driving can be dangerous.

The scar was from the car accident when he was seventeen. He was the only survivor of that accident. The familiar ache in his chest accompanied the memories. He tried not to think about it too often, saving his grief for the cemetery on the anniversary and focusing on his job instead.

He had clawed his way back to normality back then. He'd learned how to cook nutritious food, he'd taken jobs to pay the bills so he wasn't relying on his parents' life insurance. He'd put himself through the Fairyland intern program. He'd made it on his own.

He'd get through this too, whatever it was. He was a survivor, he was strong. He didn't need to let his emotions rule him. He knew how to handle anything, and look after himself in the process.

He just had to focus on what was important.

He caught sight of the Fairyland signs as he approached and some of the tension eased off his chest and shoulders. Fairyland had given him a good life, as long as he was there, he could handle anything.

And as for all the rest? He could take baby steps. One: park the car. Two: get into the park. Three: change into costume.

Four: get through the day as best he could.

28 /NATE

NATE'S PHONE RANG AS HE GOT OUT OF THE SHOWER. HE DASHED across the apartment to pick it up. "Yeah?"

"Is that really how you answer the phone?" Charlie said.

"Yes? At least it is when I can see it's you calling." Nate realized he was dripping on the carpet so he darted back into the bathroom and rubbed himself down with a towel.

"You're going to have to start being more polite, you know."

"And why on Earth would I have to do that?" Nate went through to his room and sorted through the clothes piled up on the chair, looking for a clean pair of underwear. He frowned. He really needed to get laundry done sometime soon.

"I was wrong the other day. *Now* you've arrived."

Nate groaned. "Don't tell me. I'd rather just forget the whole thing," He found some boxer briefs and pulled them on one-handed.

"Well that's just too bad, no one's going to forget what you did. And why should they? It's media gold! You've basically gone viral, my good buddy."

"But I was just–" Nate sighed, tried to gather his thoughts. "I just want to be Prince Valor, not some weird hero."

"Can you hear yourself? Prince Valor *is* a hero, and after

yesterday you're gonna have a ten-year contract to be him. Maybe longer, if you keep your looks. Management notices this kind of thing."

Nate huffed a little in response.

"I'm picking you up, be downstairs in five."

Charlie ended the call and Nate hurried to pull on clean jeans and a T-shirt. Or, clean enough, anyway. He ran downstairs and met Charlie just as he pulled up outside.

"Superstar!" Charlie cried as Nate climbed in.

"Shut up. You of all people have to treat me like normal, okay? Not negotiable," Nate said. "But thanks for picking me up."

"Okay, okay. I mean I don't want you to get a big head – you won't fit into your special-event crown." Charlie handed Nate his phone. "Look at the social media coverage for a second. There's a particularly great picture of you and the little girl everyone's resharing."

"Do I have to?" Nate looked at the phone with some trepidation – he hadn't been joking when he'd said he didn't want to be a hero. He'd felt awkward the way the people in Wardrobe had looked at him, yesterday. Up until it turned into joking anyway. He truly did need Charlie to treat him normally.

He felt totally uncomfortable with the idea of people idolizing him or treating him like he'd done something extraordinary. He didn't deserve that. Compared to Dashiel, he'd barely earned his job at all. And what had happened with Minako had been all instinct, based on his years as a lifesaver. He hadn't planned to show up Dashiel or make himself go viral. He'd just been thinking of Minako. And now? All he wanted was to disappear behind Prince Valor.

Charlie finally picked up on the seriousness of his mood when he handed his phone back without saying anything. He changed the topic of conversation.

"So, the Forest Kitchen's bringing in Halloween cookies," he said. "First time ever. And they're letting me pitch some shape and design ideas."

"That's awesome, man," Nate said, the tension easing out of his shoulders. "You deserve to design the whole range. It's about time they gave you some credit."

He couldn't describe how good it felt to think about someone other than Dashiel or himself for a while, so Nate grilled Charlie about his cookie ideas for the rest of the drive in.

Once at the park, Nate's morning was routine. Except that by the time they were assembling fully costumed in the airlock, Dashiel hadn't said more than two words to him. A mumbled 'Good morning,' was all he'd gotten.

Lennon addressed all of them, Cody included. "The Reflecting Lake has temporary railings and we're back there this morning."

"For real?" Nate asked. Fairyland really was magic if they'd managed to pull that off overnight.

"Yes, to make the most of the hype. Haven't you seen what they're saying online?" Lennon said. They smiled wide and ran a hand through their hair, they looked positively giddy. "It's golden! But just in case we'll have Cody and a couple of other security personnel in attendance. I doubt anyone would try anything, but it makes sense to be safe."

"Tries something like what?" Nate felt like he'd missed something.

"People are threatening to throw themselves into the lake so you'll rescue them," Dashiel's voice had little inflection, and he gave Nate a look that was blank but also somehow hard.

Nate felt his cheeks warming. "They're joking though, right? No one would really do it."

"I think it's awesome," Ari said. She took Nate's arm and leaned against his shoulder. "I went for months solo and now I have the best Valor the park's ever seen! I'm so proud of you, and it's not even been two weeks!"

"Ari, that's sweet but–"

"Let's get out there," Neve said, cutting over Nate. She listened to her earpiece. "Cody, front or back? The other two are already out by the lake."

"Back," Cody said. "You lead."

"No rowdy queues today, we're going to ensure that," Lennon said as they moved out. "Everyone smile!"

There were two notable differences at Reflecting Lake from the day before: a white 'do not cross' line had been painted on the cobblestones, and there was a temporary safety rail made of scaffolding pipes lining the edge of the platform.

True to word, two people in security uniforms were stationed in the encounter zone, one at each end of the new security railing. The queue was huge, and for the first time, Nate could really see that they were excited to meet *him*.

The guests were friendly – lots wanted photos with Nate and lots mentioned his daring rescue. Nate smiled for so many photos and selfies that his cheeks started to ache. He really had to focus on keeping his posture upright and remembering to be positive when he spoke. It was *exhausting*.

Despite what he and Dashiel had said to each other the night before, they interacted hardly at all during the meet and greet. And when Ari and Nate bunched up with Greer and Dashiel for a group photo, Dashiel stayed on the far side of the group and didn't meet his eyes. His stomach twisted, whatever had happened the night before, it was clear Nate had succeeded in pushing Dashiel away from him.

It was Greer and Ari who kept the conversation flowing with the guests, and Nate had to force himself to focus on them instead of obsessing over Dashiel.

Back in the changing room, Nate swallowed his nervousness and tried to start a conversation.

"That went well, I thought," he said. Dashiel didn't even look at him. "Don't you think, Dashiel?"

"Sure," Dashiel said. He picked up his phone and turned

away, focusing on the screen. Nate's stomach dropped. He could take a hint. He didn't try to talk to him again.

Nate hadn't been aware of just how much he and Dashiel talked between encounters until it was gone.

It wasn't exactly deep all the time, but Nate was used to the conversation. Now it seemed like Dashiel was cold-shouldering him, and the changing room seemed both gigantic and way too quiet.

Had their almost-kiss the night before really upset Dashiel this much? His stomach turned over unpleasantly, he shouldn't have gone over there and been all into him. He shouldn't try and pursue someone who didn't want him, who was clearly trying to ignore him. It was Nate's fault Dashiel was so upset.

At least Tristan and Eric would be in before the parade. They'd both talk to him.

Nate sighed, moved to his station and sat down to have a drink. Maybe Dashiel would sort himself out and start talking to Nate again.

Yeah, right… and maybe Dracine Jones' playboy son Maximillian would come in and put on the Treasure the Unicorn costume and meet some park guests.

At the end of an exhausting day Nate got a ride home with Charlie. He practically collapsed into the passenger seat and didn't say anything for five minutes, so Charlie prodded him.

"What's up, superst– uhh, buddy? You don't look happy."

"It's nothing," Nate leaned his head back against the headrest.

"It's not nothing. And lucky for you, it's beer o'clock." Charlie drove them to their favorite bar. It wasn't exactly a fancy place, but it was comfortable. They both liked to sit up at the bar in the corner and watch people coming and going. Charlie bought a large beer for Nate and ginger ale for himself.

"You should be on top of the world, Nate. The social media alone has guaranteed you a raise as soon as you're eligible. If this hype keeps up there'll be Valor merchandise, a dedicated photo filter, all sorts of stuff. So, what's the problem?"

"It's Dashiel," Nate said. He took a deep drink of beer.

"Oh. Dashiel," Charlie said. He took a drink, too. "What's he done now?"

Nate hesitated for a minute before conceding that Charlie was bound to get the truth out of him, anyway. "Okay, so I went around to his place last night."

"Why'd you do that?"

"Because!" Nate shouted, realizing that his tone was all off. He cleared his throat and spoke more softly. "I wanted to clear the air. I thought it went well, like, we talked about some deep stuff. But then we nearly kissed again. And before we could talk about it, he kicked me out."

"Okay so, 'no kissing' is the message there."

"Yeah. And then today he just ignored me." Nate stared into his glass.

"He ignored you?" Charlie said. "But you work together, right?"

"Yeah. Usually we talk between going out to the park, or he checks in on me or gives me feedback. Today there was nothing. He just went into the changing room and played games on his phone. It was like I wasn't even there."

"Well, at least he isn't confusing you with his raw animal magnetism?" Charlie grinned like this was funny.

Nate kicked the bar with his foot. He was probably pouting, he was feeling that disgruntled. "The raw animal magnetism doesn't go away just because he isn't talking." He mumbled.

Charlie shoved him in the arm. "What do you want to happen then, buddy?"

Nate sighed and drained his stein, then paused to burp before he answered.

Charlie snorted. "Well at least there's no danger of anyone mistaking you for the real Prince Valor."

Nate rolled his eyes. "There's no point talking about what I want to happen," he said. "What I want isn't going to happen, so it doesn't matter."

There was a short break in the conversation. Charlie frowned as he thought, watching a couple come up to the bar and order their drinks before replying.

"Tell me. Tell me or I'm going to make you eat a whole plate of jalapeno poppers."

"That's not a threat, jalapeno poppers are delicious," Nate raised an eyebrow.

"What if I cover them with the strongest hot sauce, extra hot?"

Nate pulled a face. "Okay fine, but you can't laugh at me. And you'll have to get me another beer."

"As you wish," Charlie said. He turned to gesture at the bartender for another round.

"I want to kiss him again," Nate said. Then he closed his eyes and covered his face in his hands.

Because what kind of person wanted to kiss someone who'd treated them so horribly?

Charlie patted his back. "Hey, that's not impossible, and to be frank, not entirely unexpected. It happened once, it almost happened last night. It seems like he's into it as well."

"Except he's not as well. I'm not about to push my affections on him, that's totally gross." Nate dropped his hands and looked at them. "He said it couldn't ever happen. That we're banned from dating by Fairyland rules."

"So the fuck what?" Charlie pushed the new beer stein towards Nate. "As long as it doesn't interfere with your performance on the job, it shouldn't matter, right?"

"Yeah, well... tell that to Dashiel."

"Maybe I will."

"–No, don't," Nate shook his head. "There's no point. He's all by the book and doesn't break the rules and there's no other way."

"But what about what you want? You deserve good things."

Nate stuck his tongue out at Charlie. "I just want to do my job and get paid and do okay."

"Well, you're doing brilliantly, and guess what?"

"What?"

"You're also a great guy and you deserve love."

Nate looked at him for a moment and then smiled. His heart warmed with affection for his best friend. They'd been through so much crap together, and Charlie always seemed to know exactly what he needed. "You deserve love, too, Charlie." Nate sighed. He didn't see any solution to what was going on with Dashiel, so what was the point of talking about it? He took another drink.

"How was your day? How's *your* love life going? Any likely prospects on the horizon?"

"There is no love life." Charlie chuckled and drank his ginger ale. "And don't try to change the subject, we're talking about you."

"There's nothing to talk about."

Charlie took a deep breath. "Okay. Then imagine something for me. In a perfect world, where there's no Fairyland rules and no restrictions, and you can do and have whatever you want..."

"Uh-huh?" Nate had half closed his eyes so he could more easily imagine this world.

"What would you do?"

"Well first, I'd buy all the newest game consoles on the day they come out and I'd play them all the time," Nate said. "Nothing else. I mean, I assume in this ideal world I'd have a lot of money."

"Sure, okay. But when you're done playing games all day would you want to be with his royal capriciousness?"

Nate thought about it hard. *If I tell Charlie I want Dashiel, would Charlie do something crazy like talk to him?*

Probably not, right?

And even if I do like him, do I really want to date someone who thinks just straight up ignoring people is a reasonable way to act? Do I want to date someone who yells at people and doesn't talk about his feelings? Do I want to date a tall, strong, handsome hero who could probably easily carry me in his arms if I pass out?

Yeah.

Nate sighed, goosebumps prickling his arms as he thought about it.

Do I want Dash? Fuck yeah, I do.

"Yeah. Yes, I'd be with Dash and we'd live in his apartment with the gorgeous view and he'd cook for me and I'd make him laugh – and his smile is so gorgeous – and he'd chill the fuck out and we'd kiss and he'd be gorgeous and dreamy and it'd be electric and we wouldn't have to worry about anything because I'd be a world-record holding *Princess Honesty's Game* speedrunner."

"Thought so," Charlie said. "Sheesh, you've really got it bad."

Nate looked into his face, trying to read his expression, but everything had gone a bit muzzy from the beer buzz.

"But don't you dare do anything stupid, Charlie."

Charlie took a sip of his ginger ale. "Don't you worry your pretty little crowned head, Your Majesty. I won't."

29 /DASH

DASH CONTINUED NOT TO TALK TO NATE IN THE CHANGING ROOM ON Friday morning. He told himself that it seemed to be going well. Nate had said good morning to him, and Dash hadn't responded – though the hard lump in his throat had urged him to, and then Nate had sighed and walked away.

Hearing his sigh hadn't been pleasant. There was a tightness in Dash's stomach after he'd heard it like he'd eaten a bad burrito, and his Nate-related hearing seemed to be heightened. Dash heard every noise Nate made in the changing room, whether it was the moving of a chair, the rustle of clothes or Nate taking a drink of his massive coffee. It was very distracting, and Dash couldn't concentrate properly on the Build Your Own Fairyland game level he was trying to beat.

But on the upside, at least the two of them weren't kissing. Or almost kissing.

He wondered if what he was feeling for Nate was so overwhelming because he liked him, or because he'd be been alone for so long. It had been a dry spell, and since his parents had died, he had just found it... difficult to connect. Really the only person who had been able to reach him was Greer, and even she had struggled.

Nate got changed into his Prince Valor costume, and Dash definitely did not half watch in the corner of his mirror. That's when Lennon came in.

"Hey Dash, can you come outside for a moment?" they said.

Dash glanced at Nate. This had to be about the float. He looked away quickly when he met Nate's eyes.

"Sure, Lennon." Dash followed Lennon out into the airlock. Once the door had closed and he was sure Nate wouldn't be listening he asked. "What's up? Did you want feedback on Nate?"

"Not until Monday, today still counts as part of his trial period."

"So, what is it?"

"Someone to see you. Said it was urgent." Lennon pointed to the window that showed the path connecting the airlock to the behind-the-scenes zones of the park.

A redheaded man stood there. He had a staff lanyard around his neck, a Fairyland-branded reusable soda sipper and a Forest Kitchen uniform partially covered with a grey hoodie.

"Umm, Lennon? Who's that? And why does he want to talk to me?" Dash asked.

Lennon frowned and their eyebrows drew together. They made a non-committal noise, then turned and went into their office.

Okay, so they were no help.

He glanced at Cody, who was watching him with some amusement.

"Do you know who that is?" Dash asked him.

"I have an inkling," Cody gave him a smile that was all even white teeth and a little intimidating. "Go on, he's staff, he's safe."

"That doesn't necessarily follow," Dash grumbled. He felt very uncertain, especially after Cody's sharkish smile, but he went outside to the path anyway, walking a slightly less pronounced Prince Justice walk to give himself confidence. Because what else could he really do?

"Dashiel, right?" The redhead guy said as soon as he emerged. "You asked to see me?"

"I'm Charlie," Charlie said. He switched the cup of soda to his left hand went to shake Dash's. "I work at the Forest Kitchen but, more pertinently, I'm Nate's best friend."

"I've heard of you," Dash said. He swallowed, uncertain. He shook Charlie's hand. "What's this about?"

They were still shaking hands – Charlie's grip was warm, firm but not intensely hard – when Charlie responded.

"I need you to stop being a dick."

"Uhh, what?" Dash's brain was having some trouble processing. The friendly greeting, the handshake, he genial way Charlie had said that to him. It didn't compute. What kind of man introduced themselves to someone and then immediately told them to stop being a dick? And he hadn't even said it in an angry way.

"You heard, I think. I said stop being a dick."

Dash shook his head. "Wait, what? Why?"

"Look, Nate and I talk a lot."

"So I heard." Dash rubbed the tiny hairs on the back of his neck.

"Okay good. You're really doing a number on him. And that's not cool."

Dash's stomach dropped. He wasn't comfortable with this conversation. At all. In fact, he'd spent most of the last couple of days trying to avoid conversations like this entirely. He crossed his arms and frowned. "I'm not sure this is any of your business."

"Oh, and I agree – it's totally not. But you *made* it mine the moment you decided to mess with my best friend," Charlie said. He sighed and looked away into the distance. Dash could easily imagine him as a farmer, looking over his fields at a particularly nasty bank of clouds. "See, Nate's a great guy. He's kind of a mess sometimes but he's the most genuine person I know. You know? What you see is what you get with him, and he'd never play games or lie to look good or whatever. But you? You're all over the place."

"Excuse me?" Dash bunched a fist by his side, his nails digging into his palm. Charlie held up a hand.

"Not done. One moment you're yelling at him, then you're kissing him, then the next you're pretending he doesn't exist."

"–Keep your voice down!" Dash's heart raced. If Charlie knew that Dash had kissed Nate, then maybe other people knew too. And if other people knew then it'd eventually get to someone who took the rules seriously and Dash would lose his job. He couldn't lose his job – he'd worked too hard to get here. "Does anyone else know?"

"No, no one knows," Charlie said. "Just me, and I don't care. Except I do care that Nate's about to lose his head and it's because he thinks you're amazing but you're being a total jerk."

Dash swallowed down a moment of panic. His mouth had gone totally dry.

"Now, I don't see it myself. I mean... you do kind of look like Captain America, but you're *so* not my type. Whatever. What matters is that you're hearing me."

Dash knew he should respond but he was at a loss for what to say. "Um? I'm not actually, entirely sure what it is you're here to say to me. Unless you're trying to intimidate me into dating your best friend."

"What I'm saying is you need to get your act together. Straighten up and fly right. I'm sure you can sort this all out and be a decent guy if you get your head out of that royal ass."

Dash blinked at him. Charlie sighed, then raised his hand. For a moment Dash flinched, thinking Charlie was going to hit him.

But surely he wouldn't?

Instead, Charlie squeezed his shoulder in a surprisingly comforting gesture. He spoke as if he was explaining something to a small child... and although it was a little condescending, Dash couldn't help but feel less alone.

"You need to decide if you're into dating Nate or not. Then, tell him what you decided so he knows. And stick to that decision and act accordingly."

"Oh," Dash said. He guessed he had been sending a lot of mixed signals. And it did seem quite simple when it was put like that.

"Yeah, you see? It's not rocket science. But I guessed that maybe you needed it spelled out by someone outside the immediate equation." Charlie let go of him and Dash rolled his shoulders.

Like I could shake off what's happening. Like I could shake Nate right out of my head.

"Well... I can try," Dash said. He thought for a minute and then had a horrible idea. "Did Nate put you up to this?"

"Oh hell, no! He has no idea I'm here. He'd hate it, he'd be mortified. But the boy's head over heels for you, I can tell. But he's also afraid."

"Afraid of me?" Dash felt awful, imagining Nate afraid of him. Although Dash had certainly given him reasons enough to be afraid.

"No, afraid of being hurt again," Charlie said. His voice was a little softer now.

"Wait, hurt *again*?"

"That's really, *really* is not my place to talk about. But look, Nate doesn't fall in love easily. Usually he's a date and done kind of guy. So, if he has it bad for you – which he does – then it's unusual. Stop fucking him around. Got it?"

Dash nodded, wondering about Nate's past and what it must mean if Nate was into him that much. Charlie had said *love*. What did that mean? They barely knew each other.

"I gotta go. Good talk. Don't screw things up any more than they already are, okay?"

Dash nodded again then he realized he should be polite and actually say something.

"Yes, it's, umm, nice to meet you, too. Good talk."

Charlie nodded, raised his soda cup like he was toasting him, and walked away.

Dash felt off footed. It was a little like the sensation of walking down steps when there was one more at the bottom than expected. He felt on the verge of falling, but what kind of falling?

What did falling mean?

Falling in love?

He leaned against a tree on the side of the path and chewed his lip.

Charlie wouldn't have have come to talk to him unless Nate really was in a spin. Had he been that affected by what Dash had done?

Had he really been a dick to him by sending mixed messages?

A second's thought confirmed that he had. He had been so wound up in his career and trying to succeed he'd got in his own way. And he hadn't even thought about how Nate might be feeling about it all. He hadn't thought of anyone's emotions but his own.

He sighed, massaging his neck again. He knew he needed to give Greer an apology. He'd been acting so obsessed and weird. And he should probably check in with Ari as well, just in case. But Nate…

What does all this mean?

How do I feel about Nate? What do I want from any of this?

Dash turned, one arm around the tree, bracing himself against it. He could see into the airlock from here. He could see Cody tossing popcorn into his mouth and blatantly watching what he was doing. He could see the door to the prince's changing room. Nate was back there, behind that door. Possibly in love with Dash.

But am I in love with Nate?

He couldn't stop thinking about Nate, that was for sure. And he did keep imagining that kiss, thinking of how he'd tasted and the feel of his body against his own. But was that just lust? If he went to a club over the weekend and hooked up with a stranger would he stop imagining Nate?

He scrunched up his nose. The thought of going to a club was a total turn off.

He turned away from the airlock just as Cody waved at him. He huffed, pulling out his phone and bringing up the saved pictures from social media. The one of Nate with Minako in his arms. He was so selfless, diving in like that. He was so kind, looking after her and handing her gently back to her father.

He flicked through to the photo of the four of them with Maia, her face beaming even though that cast must've been causing her a lot of discomfort on such a hot day.

He even had one of Nate as Treasure, and he felt a smile creep onto his face as he thought of how soft and vulnerable Nate had been with heat exhaustion. How he had insisted on taking care of him, even although it didn't make sense. How he had possibly, sort of fought Cody off so that he could be the one making sure Nate was all right.

Dash flicked through the photos again, a sinking feeling growing in his stomach.

Well, fuck.

He was in love with Nate.

30 /NATE

HE HAD A HANGOVER, WHICH DIDN'T HELP. AND DASHIEL WAS *aggressively* ignoring him now, which made it worse. Nate sighed, picked up a can of mousse and started in on his hair. And it had been a long week. Prince Valor-ing was exhausting and he just wanted to sleep. All in all, it wasn't a good Friday morning.

Lennon called Dashiel out of the room, presumably so Dashiel could give them all sorts of feedback on how poorly Nate was doing.

Their first encounter was at the Rose garden, and it was rough, the pollen making Nate's nose itch. Lennon's voice from his first day echoed in his head. *You have no body functions when you're out there.* Nate had wrinkled his nose but didn't dare to scratch it.

The queue was massive again. There was a gaggle of teenagers, possibly from the same field trip as emo and fluffy skirt from the Minako incident, but these ones were better behaved. They were all – masculine and feminine presenting alike – wearing handmade Prince Valor T-shirts. They were all different rainbow colors and they had a crown drawn on in sparkly fabric paint. Under the crown they'd written "Prince Valor is my man" and on the back, they'd written their names.

On any other day, Nate would probably have found it sweet.

Today, it was just irritating. But he had to hide it and play the part, so he pasted a smile on his face, put his arm around Ari and posed for what felt like thousands of photos.

The queue moved slowly, and Nate was always talking to people. Time dragged. Then someone came to the front of the line who Nate sort of recognized – and not in a good way. At first he thought maybe it was an ex of his, or the person he'd had a disastrous date with a year or so ago.

He swallowed as the man approached and inserted himself between Nate and Ari. "You're looking very beautiful today," he said to Ari.

Nate's eyes narrowed briefly before he remembered to stay charming.

That voice.

It's the guy who groped me through the Treasure suit to see if I had breasts.

Nate's back stiffened. He was instantly was on guard, but he kept his expression pleasant, trying to signal to Ari with his eyebrows. She didn't seem to be getting it.

"Well, thank you, kind sir, you look lovely today, too," she tilted her head to the side and smiled.

"So kind," the man said. He leered at Ari and then moved closer to her. "Sounds like you're in the market for a new prince."

"Oh, I don't know about that," Ari said with a giggle, though Nate caught the briefest glimmer of panic in her eyes. "My Prince Valor has just returned from a few months away and I'm so happy to have him back."

"Him?" The man turned to sneer at Nate. "A stuffed shirt pretty boy like that? Nah. You want a *real* man."

"A real man like you are, presumably?" The words were out before he could stop himself. He swallowed hard, trying to force his jaw to unclench and his heart to slow down.

Got to be Valor, got to be charming.

Behind the man Ari's eyes widened.

The man smirked and raised an eyebrow at Nate. "That's right, I'm the real deal. A girl like this? She needs a proper man who'll keep her warm at night."

Nate's jaw worked as he bit back a thousand different responses. None of them appropriate to his role or the park.

Focus.

"Come on, let's get a photo," Ari trilled, a little higher than usual. She pulled at the man's hand so that he was facing the right way for the camera. Nate turned as well.

The man's voice dropped lower as they all smiled for the camera. Nate ground his teeth together and he was sure that his smile must look particularly forced. "Oh I bet you look gorgeous in your knickers, princess."

Ari inhaled but otherwise didn't react. Although she probably had to put up with shit like that all the time, Nate couldn't take it. Not today. He had to do something… but what was in character? What could he do that would call this dude out, change up the situation but still be Fairyland approved? He could excuse himself and say something to Cody, but he didn't want to leave Ari alone with this sleaze.

I've got it.

"Are you, by any chance, challenging me to a duel, good sir?" Nate asked, raising his voice so that Lennon, Cody and the others could hear. Surely they'd put together that if Nate was talking like that there was something wrong.

There was a slight hush and then some laughter. The guest looked around and then turned to stare Nate down.

"Damn straight I am. You're not a real prince," he puffed out his chest and eyeballed him. Nate was relieved he was a little taller than the guest, but mostly he could only feel his blood pumping.

All the new things he'd learned since he'd started at the park, all the rage at the injustice that Ari and Greer had to put up with from creeps saying sexual stuff to them or coping a feel. All the frustration over Dashiel, and not knowing what he wanted, and feeling ignored when all he wanted was…was something else.

He clenched his jaw and reached for the hilt of the decorative sword at his hip.

Behind the man's shoulder, Ari shook her head. "Oh, now, Prince Valor! Don't be silly, I'm sure this good man doesn't want to fight with you."

"Yeah, I do!" the man replied.

Nate felt a hand on his shoulder. "Valor my friend, please be patient," Dashiel said. Nate was gently pulled back by Dashiel, who moved up beside him, addressing the man. "Please good sir, my friend Valor is very dangerous with his sword, for your own health, you must stand down."

"Ooooh, another pretty-boy prince! Bring it on, I'll beat the shit out of the both of you!" The guest put his fists up and moved onto his toes like he was going to start boxing.

Nate's blood boiled, he could feel the hilt of his sword in his hand, and he was sure he was white knuckling it.

Cody appeared beside him then, one hand firmly on the man's arm. "I'm going to have to ask you to leave with me now, sir," he said. The sir was said with so much repressed anger it sounded like an insult.

"Aww, come on, we were just playing around!" the man said, although after quickly sizing Cody up he had gone white as a sheet. Ari moved next to Nate and took his non-sword arm.

Cody moved fast, escorting the man away, another security guard flanking them on the other side. Lennon smiled wide and encouraged the next set of guests to come forward.

Ari put a hand on Nate's back. "Calm down," she whispered, just low enough for him to hear.

He glanced at her, she was already smiling and waving at the next guest.

"Valor, please," Dashiel said, loudly, making a show of it. "Spare that man's life, it's simply not worth it."

Nate cleared his throat, took his hand away from his sword and nodded. "But Prince Justice, he was rude to my fair princess," Nate said. He put his hand over Ari's where it lay on his arm. "But I thank you for intervening."

Some of the guests in line clapped. Dashiel turned to the new guests, a young mother with two toddlers. "Welcome, I'm sorry you had to see such unpleasantness."

For the rest of the encounter, Nate was extra careful to stick to scripted lines and follow Ari's lead.

Inside, he kicked himself.

He couldn't risk his job with a short temper.

31 /DASH

DASH COULD FEEL LENNON'S TENSION EVEN AS THEY WALKED TO THE airlock. Once they arrived back, Lennon tore a piece from Nate for flying off the handle.

"You don't challenge guests to duels!" Lennon shouted.

"But you should've heard what he said to Ari!" Nate said. "It was indecent, and she shouldn't have to put up with scum like that."

Dash shifted uneasily from foot to foot.

"He's been banned from the park," Cody said, walking in the door with a cheery smile.

Why did he always look his happiest when people were suffering?

"I don't care what he said," Lennon continued. "You're a handsome prince who *charms* people. You never draw your sword in an encounter, *never*."

Nate pressed his lips together, his eyes flashing with annoyance. Dash's heart went out to him.

It wasn't fair.

"For what it's worth, I'm glad you stepped in," Ari said. "I just ignore that stuff now, but Nate's right, we shouldn't have to put up with it. People shouldn't think it's okay to treat us like that. We're humans too."

"Well I do agree with that." Lennon pulled their hair out from their ponytail and sighed, running their hands through it. "But there are ways to do it. You should've signalled to one of us or Cody."

"I did signal, by saying he'd challenged me to a duel," Nate said.

"Oh yeah, I picked up on that one right way," Cody said. "You let me know he was threatening you, and that you thought there'd be a fight. It was a tight code."

Nate and Cody exchanged a pleased smile.

Dash felt a thump of jealousy in his stomach. If he didn't date Nate, would Nate and Cody hook up? Would he have to work with them dating? Just the thought made him feel sick.

"Look, you did wrong, okay?" Lennon put their hair back up. "And if Dash hadn't stepped in when he did it could've been social media suicide. You think people want to see a picture of Prince Valor with a sword at a man's throat?"

"He was a jerk!" Nate shook, his hands balled into fists. "He groped my chest when I was in the Treasure costume to see if I had breasts!" His voice cracked slightly on the last word.

Dash's stomach plummeted and he looked at him sharply.

Nate'd never mentioned that had happened, had he?

"I don't care," Lennon said. "No, I mean… I care, obviously about your welfare, but if someone took a photo like that, do you think there'd be any context to it? No. It'd be a weirdly violent image of the prince threatening to kill someone. And we can't have that – you'd be out of a job, I'd probably be out of a job. It'd be in the news everywhere."

Nate licked his lips. His eyes had widened as Lennon spoke. "I'm sorry, Lennon. I guess… I mean, I didn't think of it like that."

Dash's fingers twitched. He wanted so badly to reach out to Nate and reassure him, but he couldn't. He swallowed the desire down.

"Right. Now go rest up before the parade. And everyone –

hydrate. It's hot out there." Lennon stomped into their office and slammed the door.

Ari and Greer both gave Nate hugs. Greer gave Dash one too, and then they disappeared into their changing room with Neve. Cody waited until he was sure Lennon wasn't looking and gave Nate a high five.

"Whatever they say, I thought what you did was badass," he said.

Dash's winced a little as Nate gave Cody a quick smile and headed for the changing room, walking past Dash with his head down.

Dash gave Cody a warning look and then followed him in. No way was Cody going to muscle in on this, it should be Dash who comforted him.

"Nate... Are you okay?"

Nate sat down in a heap on the chair at his station. He pulled off the sword belt while he was sitting, which looked like it was more awkward than it had to be.

"What do you care?" Nate's tone bit into him more than he cared to admit. More than he thought possible. Then Nate sighed and rubbed a hand over his eyes, smearing his makeup. "Sorry. That was rude. Lennon was right, you intervened at the right time. I was ready to punch the fuck out of that guy."

"It's okay. It wasn't an easy situation." Dash remembered a time, early on in his career as Prince Justice, when he'd seen a park guest harass Greer, calling her a slag. In the moment he'd been uncertain of how to act, hopeless even, and he had done nothing as a result. Just frozen up until the man had gone again. It was one of the hardest lessons he'd had to learn as Justice, and now the fact that he'd decided that nothing was the right course of action, that decision felt sour in his stomach. Greer had brushed it off, of course, it was par for the course for princesses, but Nate was right. It shouldn't have to be.

He sat down next to Nate, pulling over a chair from someone else's station. "Are you all right?"

"No?" Nate said looking up at him like a wounded puppy. "I feel horrible."

"Horrible like, sick? Do you want a bucket?" Dash looked around for one, but there were only wastepaper baskets. Everything in him was screaming at him to do whatever was necessary to take Nate's pain away.

"No, like, horrible like I've screwed up. And I'm so tired, and I don't know what's going on with you, and everything's happening… it's all too much." Nate's voice hitched and he swallowed like he was trying not to cry. He sat hunched forward in his chair, his shoulders almost up to his ears.

Just like when Nate had suffered from Treasure-suit heat exhaustion, Dash's heart ached to protect him, to reach out and soothe his pain. But he couldn't… not without being absolutely certain about his feelings. He couldn't risk messing Nate up even further. It wouldn't be fair of him.

"Hey, one thing at a time," Dash said, instead of putting his arms around him. "Take a drink of water." He nodded at Nate's water bottle, and Nate picked it up and took a swig. "You can't concentrate if you're dehydrated. And it might wake you up to a little too."

Nate took a shuddering breath in and nodded, drinking a little more.

"And you don't have to worry about screwing up. You didn't draw your sword and, like Lennon said, that would've been the worst-case scenario. Everyone there saw that man raise his fists like he was gonna punch you, and they saw him escorted off the grounds. You're safe."

"I am?" Nate's red-rimmed, eyeliner-smudged eyes didn't look like he believed it.

I have to try again. I can't pretend that everything that I did was okay – it wasn't – and Nate knew it wasn't. I can still be realistic and still reassuring.

"Look, I'm not saying that's the way you should handle similar situations from now on, but it didn't go that badly. Lennon was just freaked because it could've been so much worse. And because you're their new social media golden boy."

Nate sat back in his chair, relaxing a little. "I'm not a golden boy."

"Yeah, you are." Dash surprised himself by not only meaning it, but by feeling a wave of affection for Nate as he said it, rather than the resentment he was accustomed to feeling.

"Just take a minute and chill out," Dash said. "You want me to leave you alone?"

"No," Nate said. He shifted in his seat, closer to Dash, and rested his head on his shoulder, Dash felt a rush of butterflies. "This is nice. Your voice is really soothing, you know that? It's helping me."

"Okay, I'll stay." Dash swallowed, feeling the old desire to kiss him rising again.

Not the time, so not the time. And besides, I need to do something to make up for how cruel I've been. I need to do that before I'm allowed to offer something like a kiss.

Instead, Dash gently nudged Nate's head off his shoulder and picked up a packet of wet wipes. "Clean off your face and start afresh. You've messed up your makeup."

Nate cleared his throat. "Right, thanks." He took the wipe and carefully cleaned off his face.

Dash moved back to his own seat, but watched him in the mirror, feeling warm and confused and guilty all at once.

32 /NATE

NATE SLEPT POORLY ON FRIDAY NIGHT. HE WAS EXHAUSTED BUT HE was also thinking through everything that had happened that week. That day, even. He felt like he'd been stuck on the Spaceship Mayhem roller coaster, going round and round and up and down and unable to get off and rest. He would drop off only to jolt himself awake an hour or so later thinking of Dashiel.

Why do I want him, when he's so much of everything? He's intense and serious. But I could give him so much of what he needs... And he'd laugh more and we'd eat together he'd carry me to bed and...

He'd shake himself out of that thought process and then just as he was about to drop off something else would pop up. Like that creepy guy saying stuff about Ari in her lingerie.

Or Dashiel being sweet and helping him with his makeup in the changing room.

Or Lennon yelling at him.

Or Minako falling into the lake.

There was too much in his head, too much fighting for his attention.

By morning he felt as if he hadn't slept at all, so when Lennon called he didn't feel exactly patient.

But it's not Lennon's fault I didn't sleep, he reminded himself.

"Hey Lennon," he yawned.

"Morning, Nate. How are you?"

"I'm okay. What's up? You haven't called to fire me, have you?"

"Of course not," Lennon said. "You can calm down. I'm calling because I talked to my manager yesterday. They've been watching you and Dash all week and they're still favoring you."

"Oh," Nate said. "All right."

"Well, the incident yesterday wasn't great, so they're holding back on deciding until they've had some feedback from another member of staff. But it'll all be sorted out on Monday one way or another. I'd also like to catch up with you on Monday about how things are going with Dash, Ari and Greer. If you don't mind."

"Sure, fine," Nate said. His heart sank. "That's fine. Just schedule it in, I guess."

They hung up and Nate looked around his apartment.

He couldn't help but compare it to Dashiel's. It sounded like his performance and advancement at work was in Dashiel's hands, and he was constantly being compared to him too.

Nate ran his fingers through his hair. He was screwed. Who knew what Dashiel would say in a feedback session?

Either way, it would be nice to have a tidier place to live, though.

Nate found some trash bags in the kitchen drawer and walked around the apartment picking up the takeaway containers and the empty drink bottles.

As he cleaned, he began to feel better. Lennon had said that they wanted Nate's feedback on the group as well. Maybe that was his solution. If he said he couldn't work with Dashiel anymore they might be switched on shifts. Maybe Prince Diligence or Prince Magnificence could partner with Prince Justice, and Nate could pair with the other one.

He'd only met the guys who played those characters a couple

of times, but they seemed chill. Relaxed even. Friendly and not remotely competitive – at least not in the way that Dashiel was.

Whatever happened on Monday, he had that option.

With the trash collected, he did a pile of dishes that'd been waiting and put on some laundry.

Looking around the relatively clean apartment, he felt a lot better. A tidy place to live, an out if Dashiel screwed him over anymore and nothing to do but relax for the rest of the weekend.

He lay down on the couch and looked through the social media Prince Valor tags, just so for once he would be ahead of Charlie on what people were saying about him.

Anything to keep his mind from Dashiel and what he would say to Lennon on Monday.

33 / DASH

Dash's Saturday morning routine was the same as it ever was, but he was distracted, thinking about ways he could make things up to Nate. Things he could do like bring him flowers, or wine, or chocolates. But that seemed too obvious. Maybe he could do something at Fairyland? A gesture. But he couldn't do it as Prince Justice, obviously.

He could just ask him out for a drink or a coffee, apologize and go from there. Maybe a nice dinner set up at some little place by the beach?

His entire yoga and workout routine was inundated with questions.

His smoothie at the surf cafe was interrupted by a call from Lennon about meeting on Monday for the feedback on Nate.

That shook him, setting his heart thumping and his stomach tensing.

How could he ask Nate out if he was also giving professional feedback on him? How could he possibly justify such a power imbalance? ...It was horrible.

He had a little panic attack about it and then tried calling Greer. She picked up on the fourth ring.

"Dash, what's up?"

"Hey, are you up to much right now?" He needed to see her, this wasn't an over the phone conversation.

"Actually, I was just thinking about finding something to eat."

"How about I pick you up and we go for lunch?"

"But Dash, your routine," Greer gasped. Then she laughed a little. "Whatever's happening with you, it must be *huge* to interrupt your routine like this."

"I just need to…" he trailed off, lost for words. How had Nate put it? "Blow off a little steam. Or just… run some stuff past you and get your take on things."

"Sure thing, Dash," Greer sounded surprised but pleased as well.

He picked her up a half hour later and they drove out to Marina del Rey to look at the ocean and eat burgers.

"So, this is unusual," Greer said. "What's on your mind?"

Dash took a deep breath, mentally steeling himself, and then dove into it. "I'm second guessing myself all over the place," Dash replied. "And I don't know what to do. It's about Nate."

"I kinda guessed it might be," Greer smirked. Dash looked at her sharply and she bit into her burger, her eyes laughing. Dash paused before he went on.

This isn't something I should have to ask someone. I should just know this, but I don't, so….

"I don't know. I just," Dash took another big breath in. "How do you know if you're in love with someone?"

"Oh, stars," Greer said. "Is that what the problem is?"

"Don't laugh," Dash felt his cheeks burn as he stared at his uneaten burger. "This is a real problem. I don't know what to do. I think about him all the time, and I can't just ignore him, I already tried that and it didn't work."

"You ignored him? Dash! What are you, ten years old?" Greer shook her head and stole some of his strawberry milkshake.

"I didn't know what to do! And Lennon says the decision

about the parade is down to what I say about how Nate's going. I can't say something bad about him and then ask him out."

"Yeah, but you could say something *good* about him and then ask him out, though," Greer replied.

Dash was silent for a moment.

That's what it all came down to, wasn't it? If I want to ask Nate out, it'd essentially be saying he was more important than my job.

I love being Prince Justice... I can't just willingly give up Fairyland.

"I can't date him, it's against the–"

"The rules at Fairyland, yeah, yeah," Greer said. "No one's going to fire you if you make out with Nate when you're at home."

Dash went quiet again, chewing his lower lip. It wasn't that easy though, there was no way. People would notice if they weren't bickering anymore. People would know if they were going home together and turning up together in the morning. You can't keep stuff like that secret.

Greer sighed and rolled her eyes. "Come on, big guy, you brought me here to talk, so tell me what's happening inside there." Greer reached up to tap his head gently. "It's okay, it's just me. I'm not gonna judge you. Well, apart from your ignoring Nate. I think I'm still judging you a little for that."

Dash sighed heavily and set the last bit of his burger down. "I'm not kidding about the 'how do you know if you're in love' question. I've never been in love before. I've never had a relationship that lasted longer than a couple of months. And I barely even liked those guys."

Greer exhaled and finished up her burger, balled up the paper wrapper and tossed it in the takeaway bag. "Well, I'm not exactly a world expert, but in my experience, it's like… when you think about them and you feel warm and happy. Like, Fairy Gentle's sparkles are inside you. Like, things in the world can't ever be too bad, because they're there and you're allowed to see them and talk to them and kiss them."

"That sounds very cartoony," Dash said. He thought about Nate and scanned his body for sparkles or warmth. He *did* feel nice when he thought about Nate. He didn't know about sparkles, but it was kind of warm and fuzzy feeling.

"Well, it is kind of cartoony. You get sort of goofy at the start."

"How else, what else tells you if you're in love? Something more definitive."

"Um, I guess like, you want to do nice things for them, you want to beat the crap out of people who do bad things to them or make them unhappy." He thought of the flash of rage he'd felt when Nate said that guy had groped him in the Treasure costume. He'd totally punch that guy if he ever saw him again.

"Okay, so that's starting to sound pretty familiar."

"And you daydream about being with them or having a future together. And to be honest, I know you've been thinking about Nate a lot, so I think we both know the answer to that one."

Dash licked his lips and ate a massive bite of burger. Greer let the silence stretch out, giving him time to process.

"Yeah okay. I'm in love with him."

"Good work. So, what do you need to do?" Greer nudged him in the leg.

"That's the problem," Dash said. "I don't know."

Greer stood and dusted off her jeans. "Well, you've got 'til Monday to work something out."

34 /NATE

NATE SPENT SUNDAY AT THE BEACH. SWIMMING ALWAYS MADE HIM feel more centered, more alive, less confused. In the afternoon he had caught up with Charlie for fish tacos and beers before he went home and called his mother. It was all very soothing.

But once the sun went down, Nate started to think about work in the morning. And despite all the good things that'd happened – and Lennon's assurance that he had nothing to worry about – he started to feel a slowly growing dread.

Although he slept all right, and in the morning caught the bus to the park on time, he felt dread hanging over him like a veneer smothering his ordinary mood.

The bus ran early for once, so he got to the park at the same time as Cody.

He didn't realize it was Cody roaring up on a sporty-looking motorcycle at first, not until he took off his helmet.

Cody in full motorbike leathers was all rather distracting, even with his realization about his feelings for Dashiel.

Cody and Nate walked in together.

"How was your weekend?" Cody asked.

"Oh, it was fine," Nate said. "Spent the day at the beach yesterday, that was quite soothing."

"You're lucky, having such dark skin," Cody said. "If I spent a day out on the beach I'd be bright red today. I burn so easily."

"Charlie's the same – my best friend – he's got red hair," Nate said. "I can't imagine you on the beach though, somehow."

"Hey, I can have fun, too," Cody chuckled.

"What kind of fun do you get up to, then?" Nate asked, looking at him sideways. "You have the motorbike, which makes perfect sense with your whole… thing." Nate waved a hand in Cody's direction.

Cody laughed a little. "What do you imagine I do, looking at my whole… *thing*?"

Nate gave it some thought as they passed through the staff security gates and in past the restaurants and the info center.

"I think you probably do motorbike racing through like, dangerous obstacle courses. Like, half-finished building sites and quarries and stuff." He grinned so Cody would know he was teasing.

"Yeah, that's exactly what I do," Cody said, deadpan.

Nate gasped dramatically and threw a hand to his collarbone. "I knew it."

The morning turned out strange in a few ways. Greer called in sick, so once Dashiel had come in (a little late for him, Nate thought), Lennon said Dashiel would be off the morning meet and greet.

"Since Greer's ill and I want to talk to you anyway, you can stay back for the morning. Nate and Ari can go out just the two of them with Neve and Cody."

"Sounds fine," Dashiel said, looking over at Nate. "As long as Nate feels confident enough to go out without me? Uhh, I mean, without me and Greer?"

Nate met his eyes for a moment and looked away.

What was this? Another challenge? Another freaking game Dashiel was playing, saying maybe Nate didn't have what it took?

"Yeah, I'll be fine," Nate narrowed his eyes at Dashiel suspiciously.

"Cody, can you make sure we have some extra security, please?" Lennon asked. Cody nodded and started talking into his earpiece.

Nate was already half ready, so he got into costume as quick as he could. Alone in the changing room and aware that Lennon and Dashiel were about to discuss his future, he felt horrible. As if he were on the verge of tears.

He tried to imagine himself back in the ocean. His body buoyed up by the saltwater and the rise and fall of the waves. He tried to breathe in the same rhythm that the waves on the beach. Looking up at the endless blue sky. Riding a surfboard. All those things which he'd done where he felt at peace with the world.

Nate hurried out to meet Ari, sure she'd be able to cheer him up. She wasn't in the same rush as he was of course, so he had to wait a while, but when she came out she gave him a big smile and a hug and he felt less lost.

"No drawing your sword today, remember?" Ari nudged him as they got ready to walk out.

"Without Justice there to hold me back, I could stab every creepy guy in the kingdom," Nate joked. Ari giggled but shook her head.

"Don't even say that. I half believe you'd do it."

They went out into the park, and the dread continued to hang over Nate. He did his best to work through it, to project a friendly, charming performance. It'd never been this difficult for him, and all the comments people had made to him about being 'a natural' seemed totally alien to him now.

But then he saw a familiar face in the queue. He smiled; despite all the emotions he was battling.

Minako and her father waved from halfway up the queue and

he waved back. Of course, they had to wait for the other guests, but once he'd seen them in line Nate felt ready to give a more genuine performance. He calmed down, became his cheerful and sweet self, posing for photo after photo as if it were exactly where and what he wanted to be doing.

Finally, Minako and her father both came forward. It was the first time Nate could remember him coming up with Minako instead of holding back to take photos. Minako wore a new fluffy princess dress – this time it was in the same colors as the Princess Patience dress Ari wore.

"Prince Valor!" Minako chirped.

Nate crouched down to give her a hug. "Welcome back, Lady Minako."

"I hope you didn't catch cold after last week's dunk in the lake," Ari fussed over the little girl, adjusting her skirts for her.

"Hello, Princess Patience. I'm fine!" Minako said. She turned to hug Ari as well, who laughed musically.

"I'm very glad to hear that," Nate said. He beamed as he watched the two of them together. "And it looks like you have a new dress!"

"Minako insisted," Minako's father said. Nate stood back up to talk to him.

"Thank you for bringing her back," Nate said. "I'm sorry, I don't think we've been formally introduced." Nate held his hand out to shake with him.

"Haru," Minako's father said. He shook Nate's hand warmly. "I can't thank you enough for last week, really. It was such a scary moment and you acted so quickly. Minako hasn't been able to stop talking about it – all those photos!"

"Really, it was nothing," Nate said. "It was my pleasure. All in a day's work for a prince of the kingdom."

Haru nodded, smiling. Nate felt a tug on the hem of his shirt just as Ari spoke.

"Prince Valor? The Lady Minako has something for you."

Nate turned and crouched again. "You do? You didn't have to get me anything."

"I worked hard on it," Minako said. She pressed an envelope into his hand, she'd covered it with drawings in marker pen. Pictures of rainbows and hearts and unicorns and dragons.

"Oh, this is so sweet," Nate said, feeling on the verge of tears again, but this time it from happiness, not despair.

"He'll read it as soon as we get back to the castle," Ari said, placing a hand on Nate's arm. She raised her eyebrows at Nate and he got the hint, slipping the envelope into his brocade vest.

"I'm looking forward to it. Thank you, Lady Minako," he said.

"Now let's all of us pose together." Ari fussed over Minako again, getting her ready for the picture.

Nate nodded and drew Haru in beside him. Minako reached her arms up to Nate and he picked her up, balancing her on his hip for the photo.

"You're my favorite prince," she whispered in his ear. The last tendril of dread evaporated from him, and he knew that in that photo, he'd look the happiest out of all the photos he'd taken as Valor.

Back in the empty changing room, Nate carefully unfastened the seal on the envelope and took his time reading the letter. It had obviously been dictated to Haru and then she'd colored in all around the edges.

He blinked back tears as he ran his fingers over a drawing of Prince Valor fighting a dragon.

His first fan letter, and he was sure, his most important one.

35 / DASH

DASH SAT DOWN OPPOSITE LENNON IN THEIR OFFICE. LENNON WORE A fitted pantsuit, in medium grey with a crisp white button-down shirt under it. They looked flawless. Next to them, Dash felt a little underdressed in his Fairyland summer intern T-shirt and torn jeans, but it wasn't like Lennon was going to judge him for that.

"So, you know why we're here," Lennon leaned forward expectantly.

"Yes. Are you really going to just take my word as the final decider for what happens with the new parade float?" Dash asked. He shifted in his seat, pretending that it was his physical position making him uncomfortable and not the situation itself. He was still uncertain about what he should say, and how he should say it. All the emotions he'd been feeling were tangled up, confused between how pretty and nice Nate was and everything he'd been working towards himself.

"No, it's not just your word," Lennon said. "But the feedback you give will have weight. You're a long-standing and invaluable employee."

Dash nodded. He visualized the winged horse float, how it

would feel to ride on it. The wind in his hair as he was lifted into the sky with Greer. It would be so much fun.

Then he thought about Nate, on his feet with a sword in hand, just him against a huge animatronic dragon. It would be so impressive, so dashing, and he'd be recreating one of the fan-favorite scenes of any Fairyland franchise movie.

And he would rock it.

Lennon watched him, tapping their fingers on the desk. "Anytime you're ready, Dash."

"So, it's only been a week, and I don't feel like it's a long enough time to really get a read on how he's doing. Not in a fair way, I mean, it'd be at least a month trial if it were down to me."

Lennon smiled ruefully and nodded. "Yes, if it were up to me as well. But you know how things work around here. It's either months of waiting for very little or everything changing at once."

"Yeah, of course," Dash said. This kind of thing had happened before, like with Fairy Gentle.

"And it doesn't have to be a detailed diatribe on every trait he has. I just want your impressions, broadly speaking. I know this puts you in an awkward position, Dash, but you're one of the people working closest with him. They want to start construction tomorrow on whatever float they settle on, so the time pressure is real. I've already had six emails this morning asking for my feedback."

Whatever float they settle on, Dash thought.

They really are choosing between Prince Valor and Prince Justice. Between me and Nate.

His stomach turned over. *I think I'm going to vomit.*

Dash imagined Nate in his Valor costume. He looked so handsome. And he had only been at the job a week, with minimal training, but already Dash was confident that he could go out with just Ari and be fine. He knew what he was doing. He knew the role, he knew what he had to provide to the guests. And the hiccups he'd had along the way, the times he'd stumbled? Well. If

Dash hadn't been messing with him, being hot and cold and ignoring him and nearly kissing him, then he doubted whether those stumbles would have happened at all.

How awesome would Nate look facing down the dragon? Sword in hand. He could just see him yelling up at the thing like he could tame it... like through the force of his will he could make it roll on its belly and give up the princess.

Dash had seen Nate's anger on Friday – and it was powerful. He had so much passion in him.

It was also incredibly hot.

He knew what he had to do.

He cleared his throat. "It should be the dragon," Dash said. "Without a doubt."

Lennon's eyebrows shot up their forehead like they were trying to hide in their hair. "The dragon. Really?"

"Yes," Dash said. It felt like the right thing to do. The tension in his shoulders evaporated after he'd said it. "Yes. Nate's been exemplary in his role as Valor. Especially considering how little time he was given to train up."

Lennon nodded and made a note on the papers in front of them. "I think so, too."

"Besides, it makes sense to capitalize on the excitement over him, given the rescue and everything."

"Good point," Lennon said. "But let's keep the focus on your impressions of Nate. How do you think he does in a group setting?"

"He's great in a group. He has a real knack for getting on with people, he makes them feel comfortable and they trust him almost instantly." Lennon made another note, so Dash kept talking. "He's a team player, you know? And I know he and Ari have been having a blast out there. Between him and me, we've also improvised some really cool stuff, and I feel comfortable with him by my side."

As he spoke, the truth of what he was saying settled on him. If he hadn't been trying so hard to out-do Nate at the start of the week, he might've noticed that he didn't have to. Just having Nate there made him a better Prince Justice.

"That's very high praise, thank you, Dash," Lennon tapped his pen on his notepad. "It all matches up with what Neve's said, and what I've noticed myself."

"Great," Dash said. He felt a lightness in his chest. Not the total weight of his own indecision and guilt lifting off him, but the start of something better. This was definitely the right decision.

"Okay, so any concerns about Nate?"

"I guess, just that we need to make sure he gets all the training he needs. He's so good, it might be easy to forget and just let it slide, but we shouldn't." He paused to take a breath. Lennon was blinking at him, head tilted. "I can do more one on one with him, and he'd probably benefit from some extra time with Ari and Greer as well. They have so much experience, it'd be valuable for him, I think. Maybe a round or two in the evenings or on off days with the other princes, too, so he can have a wider amount of experience."

Lennon smiled and wrote those ideas down as well. "Wow, you've really thought this through, it's useful feedback," they said.

"I really haven't," Dash said. "I've been a bit up my own ass lately, but I'm trying to fix that."

Lennon suppressed a smile and Dash tried not to feel offended by it. All that mattered now was the prince he chose to be moving forward.

"Right, well, unless you had any issues you wanted to raise, that was all I needed from you. Thank you for your candor, Dash."

"No problem, any time."

Dash left Lennon's office, feeling much lighter than when he'd gone in. He'd done the right thing, he could feel it in his soul. Now the challenge was to continue doing right.

36 / NATE

NATE'S GOOD MOOD FROM READING THE LETTER FROM MINAKO WAS shaken when Dashiel walked in and he remembered that Dashiel had probably just lost him the coolest work opportunity of his life.

Dashiel, to his credit, looked uncomfortable when he met Nate's eyes.

"How did the encounter go?" Dashiel asked.

"It was fine," Nate cleared his throat and turned away, pretending to fix his hair. He could see Dashiel in his mirror and he inevitably met his eyes.

"Cool," Dashiel said. "No troublesome guests?"

"No," Nate said. "We lucked out." The tension was killing him, and he wasn't sure at all why Dashiel was being all nicey-nice.

He slammed his comb down on his dressing table. He had to say something. "Can you please just stop being friendly and let me off the hook? I know you told Lennon I'm no good. And that must mean you're getting the new float, right? So if you want to rub it in my face, go for it, now's your chance. Get it over with."

Dashiel took a step back, looking somewhat affronted.

"I mean, I don't blame you," Nate said, sighing. He ran a hand through his hair and looked away. "I'm so new and I don't know shit about this job. You've been here for ages and you've earned it."

Silence. Dashiel shifted a little, then sighed and picked a baseball cap off his station and turned away. He cleared his throat. "I'm gonna take a walk, I'll see you later."

Nate watched him go in the mirror, his heart racing, conflicted between disappointment and frustration. He picked up his water bottle and took a drink, low-key hating himself for how he'd just acted. But it wasn't like anything he'd said wasn't true, he knew what Dashiel would have done.

The door to the changing room opened and Lennon walked in, the smile on their face broad and a sheaf of paper in their hand. They came up to his station, so he turned in his seat, wondering why they were smiling.

"Hey, Nate, good news!" they said.

"Good news?" Nate asked, confused. "I thought–" Lennon cut over him.

"–The new float in the parade is going to be the dragon, and you and Ari will be riding it! Well, she'll be riding it, you'll be in front and every now and then over the parade course, you'll kind of fight it. I mean, obviously you wouldn't *really* fight it, but it'll look awesome."

Lennon put the concept art of the dragon float down on Nate's station.

"I just made the call to the boss, and they're starting construction tomorrow." Lennon smiled and folded their arms, looking pleased and waiting for Nate's reaction.

Nate blinked at the art and then at Lennon, confusion making his heart race. "But didn't you just talk to Dash?"

"That's right, and he recommended that the dragon float goes ahead. He gave you a glowing review, lots of good points." Lennon rubbed the back of their neck. "He really likes you, I think."

Nate's jaw just about dropped to the ground.

"I'm sorry, what?" Nate said. "None of this is computing."

"Just between you and me, I think it cost him a lot to talk you up," Lennon said. "And it was hard for him, but he did it. He's not always been kind about other Prince Valors, you know. So I think this really means something."

Nate swallowed hard. "And now I've gone and fucked it up," he said.

"I sincerely doubt that you have," Lennon frowned.

"I just insulted him, basically," Nate said. "I threw it – I threw the nice thing he'd just done, his kind gesture, back in his face." He turned away from Lennon and let his head sink down onto the makeup table. His forehead pressed against the concept art for the awesome dragon float.

Lennon shook their head. "Go talk to him. The two of you need to sort out what's happening between you, anyway. I don't want it interfering with your work again."

"Um?" Nate's heart stopped for a second. He sat up again, suddenly terrified both he and Dashiel would be fired, even though Lennon appeared to still be smiling.

"You two are into each other, right?" Lennon said. "You should sort that shit out before it affects your work any more than it already has."

"But the rules…" Nate said. "Aren't there guidelines about not dating people? You told me on like, the first day. You said it could end in termination."

Lennon shrugged a little. "It was your first day, I wanted you to focus on the job, not the hot co-workers. I say that to *everyone* on their first day."

"But Dash said it, too, he said if we dated we could lose our jobs."

"Yeah, but it's not really a rule so much as a guideline," Lennon said. "The park really *would* fire you if you were kissing each other out there in your prince costumes. Outside of work, though? Your life is your own. We're not going to interfere with that."

"Right, yeah, that makes sense," Nate rubbed his forehead. He felt a headache coming on.

"And I trust the both of you to be professional and not let it affect your work, okay? More than it already has, I mean. You both gotta keep your emotions in check." Lennon patted his shoulder.

Nate chewed on his lower lip and ran his fingers over the little drawing of himself as Prince Valor, sword raised, fighting the dragon. The thought of getting to be the guy in the picture made his heart race.

All my dreams are coming true... he thought, and then he shook his head. Lennon was talking about him and Dashiel.

And the possibility of us dating.

"Yeah, it's been a bit of a rollercoaster." Nate rubbed his temples.

"I bet it has. There's an hour until the parade, so Dash should be back soon," Lennon said. "Try and relax until then. Kick back, have a cold drink. We can't have Prince Valor passing out."

"Thanks, Lennon."

Lennon waved as they headed out of the changing room and the door swung shut, leaving Nate alone. It was sort of eerie without anyone there, all the costumes hanging limp on their hangers. He hoped Eric or Tristan would be in soon. Maybe he should go hang out in Wardrobe and catch up with Molly and Teddy? Regardless of the thought, something kept him in his seat.

Nate rubbed a hand over his sore, tense stomach.

What do I want? I want Dash, I know I do. But what would the future with him look like? And what would be best for me?

37 / DASH

Dash walked through the park in his sunglasses and a baseball cap so that no one would notice he was Justice.
For now, I'm a tourist. I'm going to pretend I don't know the park, and I'm going to explore. I'm here to have fun, that's all.
He was shaken from Nate's outburst, he could feel a heavy lump in his stomach which the exchange had put there. He needed some time to process what had happened.
He took his time, exploring the bits of the park he didn't spend much time in. The Pirate's Cove, with its harbor that was really just another bay of the Reflecting Lake, the employees dressed as friendly pirates greeting guests and making jokes with them. The Pirates got to be a bit more teasing, even bordering on rude compared to the princes and princesses. It did look like fun, but Dash would never trade his role as Justice for anything.
He took a ride on the swinging pirate ship and got into a fun screaming contest with the kid sitting on the opposite deck of the ship. The kid would scream when their side of the ship was at the top of the swing, and when Dash's side was up at the top he'd shout as loud as he could. Yeah, he was risking going hoarse before the parade, but he didn't care. Besides, everyone was laughing and joining in. He felt giddy after the ride like he'd

shouted out all the air in his body. He was light-headed, but in the best kind of way.

Almost feels like I'm on vacation here.

After, he took some time to look through the gift shops. He almost never went into the gift shops unless there was a staff sale. He took his time, perusing the pirate stores and then moved back towards the Enchanted Forest section of the park. This was where the Treasure things were, and the Prince and Princess merchandise.

His heart skipped some. This shouldn't be hard, but with everything he'd been feeling lately, maybe it wasn't a surprise that this made him emotional, too.

I haven't bought myself anything for a while, he thought. He was restrained about buying merchandise for himself, he didn't want to fill his apartment with clutter. He usually waited for the classiest limited editions, the collector's items.

Because I'm a pretentious idiot. I could just buy things because they make me happy. Now that was a revolutionary thought. How often did he do things to make himself happy and not just because it was efficient or necessary? The wander around the park had unlocked something inside him, opened him up to fun. Or maybe that was Nate's influence?

He looked through the T-shirts and the little plush toys of the characters. In one aisle against the wall there were some bare shelves and display space, and as he wandered past a shop worker brought in a large cardboard box.

"What've you got there?" Dash asked.

The worker set the box down and looked up at Dash. Dash took in his staff lanyard and gave him a smile. Their badge read 'Sal'.

"New Prince Valor and Prince Justice merch. You know that range that came out for the princesses last month? It's their side of the same line."

"Oh, I didn't see the last range."

"Just there, behind you," Sal nodded. Dash turned to see a collector's grade range of collectibles – not the kind of thing that they sold for kids to play with, but for the adult fans with disposable income. The people who liked quality and didn't mind paying for it. Dash's heart jolted - exactly the kind of thing he'd love to own.

Little porcelain figurines of each of the princesses, each dress lovingly hand painted.

A range of jewellery with little tokens for each of the characters. Necklaces, cufflinks, brooches, earrings and charm bracelets. It was lovely stuff. Really well designed and made with gold and silver and sparkling crystal accents.

Dash picked up an enamel pin with a stained-glass image of Princess Patience on it, edged in gold with a little dragon dangling off the bottom on a piece of gold chain.

He turned to watch as Sal unpacked some of the new things. "Is there one of these, but for Prince Valor?"

Sal squinted at what Dash was holding and nodded. "Yeah, I think so. Just a second." She pulled a few handfuls of stuff out of the box and then came up with an enamel pin in a crackling plastic bag. "Like this?"

Dash took it off her, his breath catching in his throat. It was perfect. A heroic-looking Valor in portrait. Dash suspected he was positioned so he'd be looking at Patience if you bought them both. The design really made the blue of his tunic pop and he suited the stained-glass effect.

He ran a fingerpad softly over the lines of the pin, feeling the smooth enamel and the ridges of the pattern. Valor deserved someone wonderful, and here he'd been such an ass to him. Maybe, just maybe, he could be the person Valor - no, Nate - deserved.

"Are you sure you don't want a Prince Justice one?" Sal asked, having excavated some more pins from the box. Dash looked at her, surprised, and she winked. "Just a hunch."

Dash smiled and nodded, taking one of those as well. "That's perfect, thank you so much."

He took them up to the counter, and on impulse he also took a little Treasure the Unicorn plushie from the box beside the till.

He went back to the Enchanted Forest staff changing rooms, swinging his bag in one hand and whistling. He felt lighter, excited, but with each step closer to the Airlock the nervousness rose in his stomach. He started thinking of reasons why he shouldn't do this. What if Nate turned him down? He'd be heartbroken, how could he come into work tomorrow?

What if Nate reported him and he lost his job? Then he'd be heartbroken and unemployed.

He ignored the uncertainty and kept walking. He wouldn't back down.

This isn't going to be easy, he thought. Nate had sounded so… tired, the last time they'd talked. Tired and angry. And yeah, it hurt that he'd accused him of sabotage, but Dash didn't blame him in the least for it. All Dash had done was screw things up over and over, there was no reason for Nate to think Dash would do anything nice or kind for him.

Well, Nate, that's all about to change.

Dash straightened his back as he went into the airlock, and nodded at Cody who gave him a wave back even although he looked surprised. Dash paused at the door to the prince's changing room and took a breath, steeling himself for maybe the scariest thing he'd ever made himself do in his life.

Cody cleared his throat. "You got this, bro," He called from the other end of the airlock.

Dash glanced at him, decided he didn't want to know what Cody thought he was referring to and pushed the door open. The less he thought about how much Cody saw around this place, the better.

Nate was half dressed, in his Valor pants and pulling on his white shirt. Dash drank in the sight of his abs and his gorgeous brown skin.

The things I could do to you if you'd be willing to let me.

"Nate, I have—" he broke off. His voice had given out – it must have been from all his pirate ship shenanigans. Nate looked over, surprised. Dash's heart thumped like he was having cardiac arrest and his mouth was dry and scratchy. He couldn't back out now, though. He had to do this. "I have something for you."

Nate gave Dash a half smile and kept doing up his shirt. "It sounds like you've already done enough," he said. Dash's heart just about jumped out of his chest, but Nate's tone was soft, like, *good* soft. Not angry soft. Not *'please leave me alone'* soft.

Or was it?

"I- I don't know what you heard," Dash said. He looked at the ground, then realized he was being a coward again, so he lifted his chin, took a breath and approached Nate. "But the first thing I have to say is I'm sorry. I've treated you like garbage – and for no real reason. Well, one reason. I was scared."

Nate stopped buttoning his shirt with two buttons to go and dropped his hands down to his sides. He frowned, which wasn't the right expression for Nate to have – now, or ever. It made Dash sad to see him frowning. Nate should be happy.

"Scared of losing your job?"

"Yes, a little. But I think that was an excuse because I was mostly scared of letting you get close to me. I was scared of how I feel when I'm around you." Dash could feel his cheeks warming. He never blushed. And he sounded like the romantic lead in a movie, like someone had written these cheesy lines for him to say. But he meant them, too. And Nate didn't seem to be hating it.

"And how do you feel when you're around me?" Nate's voice had got a bit huskier, charged with anticipation.

"I feel like…" Dash huffed his breath out and tried to think of the right words. "Like none of what I usually worry about matters."

Nate tilted his head to the side. "Umm, okay?"

"Because, well, usually I'm worried about what I've eaten or how much water I've drunk or whether or not I've done enough reps at the gym. I worry about how people photograph me when I'm out there as Justice, and what they're going to say about me in the comments and the hashtags. I worry about how to be the best. Well, I guess that's all obvious." Dash cleared his throat and forced himself look Nate in the eyes. "But when I'm talking to you, or being Justice alongside you, I just think about how you make me feel. It's like... like I don't have to try as hard because when I'm with you maybe I'm already good enough."

"You are good enough," Nate said. "I thought I said that the other night."

"You did, but I wasn't really ready to hear it then," Dash sighed. "That stuff you said to me the other day, some of it was the first time I can remember anyone saying it to me. Ever."

Nate shook his head, his shoulders rising and falling like he'd comically emphasized the gesture, but he was smiling at the same time. "Okay so, you're sorry. And I forgive you."

"And there's something else," Dash said. He shoved his hand into the bag and pulled out the Prince Justice pin. He'd meant to give Nate the Valor one but maybe this one was better? It depended on how Nate reacted to what he was about to say.

His heart raced like he was at the top arc of the pirate ship swing. The moment when you felt weightless and sure you were about to fall out and crash to Earth. "Nate, I really like you. In fact, I think... I think that I'm falling in love with you. And I'd really like to kiss you again, and maybe make you dinner sometime, and take you to the movies or something..."

He thrust the pin towards Nate, who was staring at him wide eyed. He took the pin and ran his fingers over it.

"Wow, this is really beautiful, is it new in?"

"Yeah," Dash said. He felt like he was far away from the conversation suddenly. Had he said all that stuff about his feelings, or had he just imagined it? Nate wouldn't ignore that, right? He'd say something, surely... he wouldn't just leave him hanging like this? "So um, what do you think?"

Nate looked up from the pin, set it down and nodded, chewing his lower lip for a moment. "You did treat me like garbage, Dashiel. So I don't really know what to think."

There was a pause, and Dash held his breath as his heart came plummeting back to earth.

Then the worst thing Dash could have imagined happened. Nate shook his head, put down the pin on his makeup station and walked out of the room.

Dash's heart melted into a puddle when the door closed behind Nate. And although his instinct was to freeze up and give in, he realized that he couldn't just let him walk away. Not without knowing what Nate's answer was for certain.

If Nate was going to turn him down, he had to say it out loud. He had to be explicit, and Dash had to know for sure that there was no hope. He ran after Nate, who had walked straight through the airlock and out the door, onto the wooded path to the park. The same place he'd talked to Charlie.

Dash ran fast his pulse beating in his throat. He really had to catch Nate now – because if Nate went out into the park half dressed, he could totally lose his job.

"Nate!" he called, once he was out of the airlock.

"I need to think!" Nate called over his shoulder. Lennon's comments about letting their personal feelings effect their work echoed through Dash's head. Now Nate was halfway up the path, skirting the edge of the Haunted Tree Ride.

"Come back," Dash panted. He put on an extra burst of speed on and caught up to Nate grabbing his arm and turning him.

"You need to give me a second," Nate was angry now, his eyes flashing. Dash recognized it from Nate's duelling incident with the rude guest. "You can't just spring stuff like that on me. Like you're all sweet now and I should forget all the stuff that happened. And let go of my arm!" Nate tugged his arm out of Dash's grip. He hadn't meant to hold onto him that long.

"S-sorry."

"And what, are you going to turn over a new leaf? Are you just going to forget about who gets the most likes on Instagram? Or are you still going to get all weird about who gets the bigger stocking at Christmas time?" Nate ran a hand through his hair. "How much am I expected to put up with here?"

"No – no, I won't be like that," Dash said. "I'm going to try, and yeah, maybe I will mess up and get competitive sometimes. But I don't want to. I want *you*."

Nate looked him in the eyes, his eyebrows drawing up and wrinkling his forehead. His jaw worked like he was chewing on jerky.

"I thought I wanted you, too," he said. "But maybe... maybe that's a bad idea for *me*." He turned to go. "Give me a minute."

"No, you can't," Dash lunged forward and took his hand, pulling him back.

"Not everything happens on your schedule!" Nate protested.

"You're not dressed," Dash said. "You're in the pants and boots but just a shirt – you can't go out where people will see you."

"Oh," Nate looked down at himself. "You're right." Then, inexplicably, he started to laugh. A proper giggle.

"And I hear you, I hear all your concerns," Dash said. Nate's giggle had given him hope, and the hope gave him the confidence to try to placate him again. Dash still had the shopping bag in his other hand. "I'm sorry, I'm an ass. But please, will you consider, this?" Dash pulled the Treasure plushie out of the bag and gave it to Nate. "I'm really, truly sorry."

Nate's smile turned indulgent as he took the little unicorn and turned it over in his hands before pressing it against his own chest, right over his heart. "How many apology gifts do you have in that bag?"

"There's just one more thing... but I was hoping I could keep it for myself," Dash said. He slowly drew out the Valor pin and showed it to Nate. "But it kind of depends on your response. If you, um, if you don't want to have anything to do with me, I understand and you can keep all the presents. But maybe, if you say yes, I can keep this one."

"You two, get back inside!" Cody called from the door. "You're supposed to be getting ready, Lennon says!"

Dash nodded and tilted his head at Nate, who led the way back into the changing room. They didn't say anything as they walked, and Dash gave Cody his best quelling look. He suspected it wasn't very impressive, due to how his entire body was waiting on edge for Nate's answer. His fingertips were tingling, and his breath was short.

How do people in romantic movies do this stuff without passing out?
Oh right, they're fictional characters.
I hope I don't pass out.

Once they were back in the changing room, Nate looked at the plushie unicorn and gave it a little kiss on the nose. He set it down and gave Dash the cutest little shy smile he'd ever seen.

"You know... that day, when I was Treasure, you took really good care of me." Nate swallowed, and Dash distracted himself watching Nate's Adam's apple bob up and down. Even his Adam's apple was adorable. "So, I guess... What exactly are you suggesting?" he asked, taking a step towards Dash.

"Will you, please, be my boyfriend?" Dash asked, somehow out of breath all over again. All this talking and wishing was a good workout, he'd probably be able to skip the gym.

"Even though we work together?" Nate asked. He moved in closer and Dash could smell his hair product.

"Yes."

"And even though I'm a total slob and you're the most organized person on the planet, after Marie Kondo?"

"Even though," Dash said, although he privately promised himself he'd sort out Nate's apartment for him.

"Ask me again?" Nate's eyebrows drew together. He gently placed a hand on Dash's shoulder. His eyes had gone all soft and misty as he looked up at him. Dash's heart flipped and flipped again.

"Will you be my boyfriend? Please, handsome?"

Nate burst into the biggest grin Dash had ever seen. "Fuck yeah," Nate put his arms around Dash. "Now kiss me again."

And so Dash did. He kissed Nate with relief, with excitement and with the kind of unbridled joy that he'd felt a touch of when he'd told Lennon that Nate should get the float. It was the kind of joy a perfect day as Prince Justice could get close to, but never match.

He pressed his chest against Nate's and wrapped his arms tight around him.

Perfect, he thought.

This is perfect.

38 /NATE

THEY KISSED SO LONG THAT THEY HAD TO HUSTLE TO GET READY FOR the parade. At least Nate was partially ready, but Dash was still in his track pants. Nate quite liked the way he could feel Dash's body through the thin material, but they couldn't get totally distracted – not when there was a show to put on.

"Here, let me help," Nate said. He went to tug Dash's T-shirt off him, but then he was right there with Dash's bare chest and he had to run his hands over it and then they were inevitably kissing again.

Finally, Dash pulled away with a reluctant expression and shuffled a few feet away so they weren't in danger of so much touching.

As they finished up, Nate had to ask. "What changed your mind?"

"About what?" Dash looked over from gelling his hair just so.

Nate walked over to Dash's station and leaned against it.

Within touching range again. Kissing range.

"About me, about dating someone from the park," he asked.

"Well, let's see," Dash said, smirking a little. "A couple of people had some stern words with me, opened my eyes a bit. And then I weighed up what really matters."

"Uh-huh?" Nate said, grinning. He knew what Charlie could be like when he had a bone to pick.

"And I decided that *you* matter, I guess," Dash said, his cheeks turning a delicate, and very fetching pink.

"You guess?"

"That you matter more," Dash amended.

"But the rules, the risk, *the job*," Nate said, prodding him in the shoulder, unable to help touching him.

Dash shrugged and sighed like he was letting go of something. "I decided you were worth it. The risk, I mean."

Nate felt a warmth spread over his chest and up to his cheeks.

It was like something had unlocked inside Dash, and he was showing this soft underbelly the world never got to see.

Like a stray cat I earned the trust of, finally. Or maybe more like a mountain lion I've somehow managed to tame.

"Aw, you're such a softie under that stern, confident facade," Nate teased, unable to help himself.

"I am not," Dash sniffed. He stood up. "And if you tell anyone anything about what I said this afternoon, I'll deny it."

"I don't think you can hide what's happened from Cody," Nate said.

Dash narrowed his eyes. "I have ways of dealing with Cody," He said. And Nate half believed it.

Nate leaned in and kissed him, reveling in the fact that he was *allowed* to do that now. Each kiss was like a little more insight into who Dash really was, and Nate loved every second of his explorations. Each kiss unlocked a little more of him. He should really put him out of his misery, though, since clearly Dash hadn't heard from Lennon that they were allowed to date.

"Best news," he said, as casually as he could under the circumstances. He turned so Dash wouldn't see the smirk Nate couldn't conceal.

"What? Me sorting myself out?" Dash asked. He squeezed Nate's hand and Nate squeezed back on instinct.

"No, but that's a close second. I talked to Lennon and they said it's really more of a guideline than a rule –the 'no dating' thing. As long as we behave in the park when we're in costume, and our relationship doesn't affect our work, there's no rule against it."

"You're kidding." Nate felt a tug on his hand and Dash pulled him sharply into his arms. Nate squirmed happily. Something about how physical Dash was with him was extremely attractive. His mind flashed to the various fanfics and dirty daydreams he'd had over the years. Maybe he could convince Dash to sneak one of the costumes home, and they could have some fun – some fanfic level fun.

He shook his head, he was getting distracted and this was important information to relay.

"Nope. It's true. You're not going to risk your job, *and* you get the boy."

Dash laughed and pulled Nate closer in, squeezing against him in a moment that left Nate breathless.

"No, I got my prince," Dash corrected. Nate blushed at that.

What if Dash is thinking similarly dirty things about the Prince costumes? No, I'm getting distracted again.

He had to be upfront about the important stuff before they discussed anything like that.

"Promise me one thing," Nate said, pulling back before Dash kissed him again.

"Sure, anything," Dash said, his expression earnest, leaning in trying to catch Nate's lips.

"Next time you don't like how something's going, you talk to me about it, instead of ignoring me for three days."

"Done," Dash said, leaning closer. Nate leaned away a little. "Just one more thing," Nate said.

"What? I just said I'd promise anything."

"Don't break my heart," Nate said. He hadn't meant to say it quite like that. He'd kind of meant to say 'don't mess me around' or 'don't play games' but, well, what he said *did* seem like it cut to the root of Nate's concerns.

Dash stopped trying to kiss Nate and nodded, looking him square in the eye. "You can trust me, Nate. I want this to work, and if it doesn't, then it won't be because I didn't try. You got that?"

Nate breathed out, the last of his concerns he had melting away. "I got it. Now you can resume kissing me again."

And they kissed until Lennon pounded on the door.

"Time for the parade, you two!"

Did you like this book? Spread some Fairyland magic, leave a review.

Seriously, please consider leaving a review. Indie novels thrive or perish on reviews so even if you just do a star rating and one sentence, it will make a big difference!

THE FAIRYLAND SERIES BY JAXON KNIGHT

Book one: Rival Princes - a rivals to lovers romance with competing handsome princes

Book two: Mischief and Mayhem - the grumpy one, the sunshine one and a roller coaster

Book three: Recipe for Chaos - a billionaire romance, featuring instalove for the billionaire and a chef who isn't impressed with money

Book four: The Good, the Bad and the Dad - the start of a sweet menage with a single dad, a handsome prince and a mischievous pirate

Novella: Tailor Made Christmas - a second chance romance featuring a tailor and a prince, set after book four

Short story: New Year's Eve, the characters from Recipe for Chaos have a night to remember

Book five: The Trouble with Order - hurt and comfort opposites attract when Link gets a new villain

FAIRYLAND BOOK 2: MISCHIEF AND MAYHEM

Mischief
    Protecting royalty at Fairyland theme park seemed about as far from Afghanistan as Cody could get. But the hot new rollercoaster brings up some unexpected trouble - and not the kind of trouble he knows how to handle alone.

Mayhem
    Dean loves running the Spaceship Mayhem roller coaster - he gets to meet new people every day! When he sees a handsome, troubled security guard repeatedly fail to ride it, he sees an opportunity to help. And maybe they can be more than friends?

Cody reluctantly accepts cute, boy-next-door Dean's help and sparks fly between them, but between mischief, mayhem and miscommunication, can they ever make a relationship work?

Mischief and Mayhem is a slow burn, opposites attract MM sweet romance featuring snark, foolishness, motorbikes, assumptions, the chicken door and a HEA
    Buy now

FAIRYLAND BOOK 3: RECIPE FOR CHAOS

The recipe is simple:
    Charlie cooks an amazing meal
    Charlie impresses heir to the theme park Max Jones
    Charlie gets a promotion and a dash of control over his kitchen

But the perfect recipe becomes unpalatable with one wrong ingredient and Max Jones is not behaving how Charlie expected...

Max is meant to inherit the entire Fairyland theme park but he just wants to party, have fun and bed as many people as possible. That is, until he meets Charlie and falls for him so hard he can't even finish the delicious meal.

Charlie doesn't have time for clubs or helicopter flights over the city, but Max is accustomed to getting what he wants, and he wants Charlie.

Featuring one part Billionaire, one part sensible chef, six cups of attraction, a generous dose of snark and a freshly prepared Happy Ever After.
    Buy now

FAIRYLAND BOOK 4: THE GOOD, THE BAD AND THE DAD

Haru is a single dad, a widower, doing his best to balance his career and raising his little girl, Minako. Thankfully Fairyland theme park is a haven for both of them. However, when both a prince and a pirate start courting Haru, his balancing act gets a lot harder...

Cillian plays a pirate at Fairyland theme park and he loves playing the rogueish character in and out of work hours. The last thing he wants is to settle down with a guy with a kid, so can't he stop thinking about handsome single dad Haru. And why can't he stop looking at pictures of Prince Magnificence and his stupid symmetrical face? And why does he keep running into both of them?

Grayson feels he's found his home in the role of Prince Magnificence, but he's more likely to run from love than seek it out. Until he meets Haru, that is. Christmas is complicated by Grayson's role being featured in a special Christmas celebration. Not only that, but his feelings for Haru, and his possible rival Cillian keep on growing. Maybe it's time to stop hiding who he really is?

The Good, the Bad and the Dad is a sweet MMM romance featuring a single father, a rogue and a trans prince with a heart of gold. No cheating, just the tentative first steps into polyamory.

Buy now

FAIRYLAND STORY: NEW YEAR'S EVE

MAX AND CHARLIE GOT TOGETHER OVER THANKSGIVING - THIS SHORT story finds them a few weeks later, celebrating New Year's Eve together with Blaze and Coco, and doing some bar hopping. But Charlie's trying to find the perfect moment to ask Max something important...

An MM short story, following on from Recipe for Chaos and The Good, the Bad and the Dad.

Buy now

FAIRLAND NOVELLA: TAILOR MADE CHRISTMAS

https://books2read.com/tailormadechristmas/

Sparks fly and old hurts flare as two men too afraid of their feelings discover some things can't be buried. Teddy loves his job working in the Wardrobe department of a theme park, but his love life needs resuscitation.

The last thing he expected was his high school best friend and crush walking in to be fitted for a prince costume. Art wants to make it big in Hollywood, and getting a job as a handsome prince might not seem like the obvious first step, but if the rumors are true it could be the break he needs. Instead, he comes face to face with Teddy, the one he left behind.

Tailor Made Christmas is a sweet second chance romance with queer characters, set in a fairy tale themed amusement park. Guaranteed HEA. Some cursing, no cheating. This is a shorter length novella style book

```
FAIRYLAND BOOK 5: THE TROUBLE
WITH ORDER
```

https://books2read.com/troublewithorder/

Opposites attract, right?

Link's past was difficult but he learned to skim through life and have things work out right, Teayang has worked for what he has and sacrificed things along the way.

When Taeyang is cast as Lord Order, the villain opposite Link's fun-loving Fairy Mischief, there's instant chemistry that can't be denied.

Outside of acting at Fairyland, Link's life is falling apart and he has no idea how to handle it alone. But years of putting up walls and projecting a happy image makes it impossible to ask for help as well.

Taeyang may love playing a villain, but in real life, he yearns to reach out to his acting partner, if he'd only accept that help... Can a villain become a friend? Or something even more?

--

The Trouble with Order is a slow burn, opposites attract MM sweet romance featuring team building, silliness, troublesome parents, assumptions, green smoothies and a HEA. It can be read as a standalone but is best read as part of the Fairyland series.

SANTA'S SACKING
AN M/ENBY SWEET WITH HEAT CHRISTMAS ROMANCE

https://books2read.com/santasacking/

Darian knew from the moment Nole Ox took over BirdTalk that their ideal job writing code for a social media platform was done.

They packed up their things and went home to Snowfall, Oregon, tail between their legs for a quiet Christmas with their folks.

However, their folks want Darian to stay busy by contributing to the community so Darian finds themself signed up to help with the Christmas pageant. Thrown in at the deep end and with only days until Christmas, their only lifeline is handsome Connor, the handsome barista-turned-handyman.

Can Darian make the sound tech work so the kids have their musical cues?

Is Connor really the perfect hunk he appears to be?

And why can't Darian just sleep in?

Santa's Sacking is a sweet, tropey Christmas story that will fill your heart and tickle your funny bone. This story is Standalone but there *may* be a return to Snowfall for next Christmas...

DASH'S CHICKEN DINNER FOR TWO

Two free range chicken breasts, or similar amount of thighs (boneless)
Half an onion – chopped finely
Two cloves of garlic (or more depending on your taste) – minced
Two heads of bok choy
Fresh peas, shelled
Packet of miso paste
Olive oil
Butter – 1 Tablespoon
Bottle of white wine

Dry the chicken pieces off with a paper towel and season with salt and pepper, set aside.

In a frying pan heat olive oil, garlic and onion on medium heat until tender, or onion is transparent.

Put a generous chunk of butter into the pan along with a glass of white wine and lay the chicken over the top of the onions and allow to cook through, turning as it browns.

Put on a half pot of water to boil with some salt and miso paste. Pull the bok choy apart and rinse before adding to the boiling water.

Ensure chicken is cooked through. Serve with garlic and onion strewn over the top.

Drain bok choy and serve next to the chicken with fresh peas. Season to taste before serving.

Drink the rest of the wine with the meal and avoid feelings as much as possible.

ABOUT THE AUTHOR

Thanks go to my beautiful wife who alpha read this book and whose emotional involvement in the characters encouraged me to continue writing.

Thanks also to Zephfi, who is the best beta reader I could dream of.

Finally, thanks to Emma. More than just an editor, Emma sprinkled Fairyland magical dust over the manuscript and elevated it to Prince levels. Best book Fairy Godmother ever.

Jaxon Knight loves theme parks, Japanese food and happy ever afters. A non-binary author from New Zealand, Jaxon spends their days writing the stories they'd like to read.

Sign up to Jaxon's newsletter to get an exclusive epilogue featuring Nate and Dash

https://mailchi.mp/6495334ea81c/jaxonknight

Find me online:

https://www.facebook.com/JaxonKnightAuthor/

https://www.goodreads.com/author/show/19244965.Jaxon_Knight

https://www.bookbub.com/profile/jaxon-knight

Printed in the USA
CPSIA information can be obtained
at www.ICGtesting.com
CBHW031447261024
16475CB00009B/257